RIDING THE ROCKET

VOLUME TWO

EASTBOUND TO KENNEDY

RIDING THE ROCKET

VOLUME TWO

EASTBOUND TO KENNEDY

T. C. DOWNER

To my wonderful family

CONTENTS

Kipling / 9

Islington / 17

Royal York / 26

Old Mill / 36

Jane / 44

Runnymede / 53

High Park / 61

Keele / 71

Dundas West / 80

Lansdowne / 89

Dufferin / 99

Ossington / 107

Christie / 116

Bathurst / 125

Spadina / 135

Kipling

"Come on, Tommy! Are you almost done? I have kids to get home to, you know," Sam shouted to me from down below.

I was still on the scaffolding, gathering up some of my tools that had fallen down. I had just started working here a week ago, and I was still getting used to how things worked. Although Sam was my friend, he could be a pain at times.

"Give me a second. I'm just picking up my stuff," I shouted back down.

Sam and I had been friends for as long as I could remember. We went to the same high school, and drifted in and out of each other's lives every once in a while. Even though we didn't see each other all the time, we always picked up right where we left off.

A couple of months ago, I had fallen on hard times. I was laid off from my job, and had been unsuccessful in finding another one. I really didn't have any skills that everyone else didn't also have, so I was really disadvantaged. Right when I was about to give up and resign myself to a life of minimum wage, I ran into Sam.

It had been about two years since I had seen Sam. In that time, he had greatly matured. We used to go to the bar and drink until closing. Now, Sam heads straight home to his girlfriend Agnes and his twins Michael and Sierra. A lot had changed in those two short years.

When I had bumped into him a couple months ago, he was on his way into the pharmacy to pick up diapers. I was on my way out, having just purchased a lottery ticket for the night's draw. As soon as we saw each other, we enveloped each other into a bear hug. He brought me home to his family, and we picked up right where we left off.

After it came out that I had been recently laid off, he told me that he was working at a construction company, and they were hiring. He gave me a good reference, and I was called in for an interview that same week. I wasn't officially hired until last week.

On my first day, I didn't heed Sam's advice on wearing old clothing that I didn't care about. I enjoyed dressing nicely at my place of work, and I didn't think a construction site would be any different. Considering the fact that I hadn't been given directions on exactly what I would be doing, I wasn't really concerned. It only took ten minutes into my work day to realize I should have been.

After that first day, I had gone home with holes in the thin fabric of my shirt, and countless stains all over my designer jeans. I was wearing those same jeans now, but had opted to borrow a more practical shirt from Sam's stash.

As I gathered the last of my fallen tools, I carefully made my way down the scaffolding until I reached Sam. As he saw me approaching, he shot me a smile and threw an air punch my way.

"Took you long enough," he said.

"Sorry. I dropped my tools," I replied.

"You mean my tools," he shot back. "Be careful with those. I won't have any more to lend you if you break 'em."

I laughed at his remark, and followed him as he walked to his truck. Although he lived in the opposite direction from where I was renting an apartment, he had offered to drive me to the nearest subway station. It was a favour that I appreciated, especially since it was a twenty minute hike to the nearest bus stop.

As he unlocked the truck doors with his keyless remote, I opened my door. Before getting in, I grabbed a sheet from the back seat and spread it across the front seat. Sam had just purchased this truck a year ago, and was still making payments on it. The last thing he wanted to do was get it dirty.

Climbing into the truck, I sank my entire weight into the seat. It felt so great to finally sit down and have something supporting my back and head. I hadn't realized how exhausted I was until I finally stopped working.

The first day left me nearly crippled; every muscle and fibre in my body was screaming in pain while being, for the most part, stuck in a very limited range of motion. It was getting better, but I was still in pain every night I got home.

I closed my eyes as he turned the key in the ignition. The roar of the engine was a welcome sound, and I lost my thoughts as my eyes slowly shut.

"Wake up, Tommy. Man, you can't really be that tired," Sam said, as he lobbed a soft punch in my arm. Although the hit would have been harmless any other day, today it sent pain ricocheting through by arm.

"I wasn't sleeping. I was just resting my eyes," I replied.

I brought my hand up to my face to wipe saliva that had slipped from my mouth. Wiping my hand against my shirt, I looked out the window at the scenery. It was really nice out here. I could picture myself buying a nice house, and settling down with a family of my own. It would be nice.

"How are you liking it so far?" he asked me.

"Well for one thing, it's harder than I thought it would be. Man, I have been in constant pain since starting this gig," I replied.

He laughed. "Don't worry. Your body will get used to it." He turned on his blinker and looked through his rear view mirror before merging into the next lane. "Do you think you'll stick around?"

I knew why he was asking me, but it hurt. Back in our youth, I had a habit of bailing on jobs after a couple of months. I would just stop showing up, and that was that. Even though I was laid off from my last job, I knew he believed that I just up and left.

"Don't worry. I'm not going to ruin your reputation, if that's what you're worried about," I spat back at him.

"Whoa, relax. I wasn't accusing you of anything. I was just asking you a question," he replied calmly. "So, do you think you'll stick around?"

"Yes," I replied, before even considering what my true answer was. Would I stick around? Maybe. I mean, I really wanted to make this work, but it wasn't all up to me.

"I'm glad," he said. A smile spread on his face, but it disappeared as quickly as it had left.

I really didn't want to continue talking about this, so I wracked my brain trying to think of something else to talk about.

"How are Michael and Sierra?" I asked him.

"Oh, my angels? They're perfect. Agnes is going out with her friends tonight, so I will have the twins to myself. They're great. I mean kids. Kids are great. You need to find yourself a woman and add some meaning to your life."

I took a deep breath, and slowly let it out. "What do you mean by that? My life has no meaning, just because I'm not hitched and have no kids?" He was starting to upset me.

"No. No, you know that's not what I meant. I mean, kids add a whole new layer of meaning to your life. You can't access it without them, you know. Trust me. It's hard to explain, but you'll know what I mean when you experience it," he replied, keeping his eyes on the road.

"Okay," I responded curtly.

"Pull your panties out of your ass, Tommy.

You know what I mean. I'm not trying to talk down to you or belittle you. I just want you to be as happy as me," he said.

I remained silent, and ignored him. If I had opened my mouth, I'm pretty sure it would have resulted in him kicking me out of his truck in the middle of the road. I closed my eyes again, and focused my attention on my breathing.

When the truck stopped, I opened my eyes. When I looked around, I realized we weren't at the subway station, but parked on the side of the street.

"Why did you stop?" I asked him. There was venom in my voice. I didn't know why I was so angry with him, but I was.

"Tommy, I'm sorry if I offended you. I didn't mean anything by it. You're my friend. Are we good?" he asked. He extended his hand towards me. I only hesitated for a few seconds before firmly clasping it.

"I'm sorry, Sam. I don't know what's gotten over me. It's just the exhaustion, you know. Everything hurts, everything kills," I replied, while bowing my head.

Sam put his truck back into drive and continued down the road. "I know. It will get better soon. You just have to believe it."

I spent the rest of the drive looking through the window at passing vehicles, and at people walking on the sidewalk. As we pulled in front of the subway station, the truck slowly came to a full stop. I opened the door, and climbed out of the truck. As I was getting ready to close the door, I looked Sam straight in the eyes.

"Hey, Sam. I just wanted to say... Thank you for being my friend," I said, as I flashed him a smile.

"Friends," he echoed. "Friends for life."

I closed the truck door and watched as he pulled away. When I couldn't see his car in the distance anymore, I made my way into the subway station. I flashed my pass at the attendant as my thighs were already pressing against the turnstile.

Standing on the platform, waiting for the train to arrive, I let out a deep breath. Today sucked, but tomorrow would be better. As the train pulled into the station, I let a smile spread across my tired face. Yes, tomorrow would be better. The train doors opened, and I plopped myself down in the first available seat. Tomorrow would be better.□

Islington

I was growing restless form standing still in one spot for such a long period of time. Mr. Tavers was making us stand in line against the back of the class until everyone remained quiet and still. After twenty minutes of trying, it didn't seem like he was going to give up.

"We'll stay here until the day is over, if that's what it takes," Mr. Tavers said, as Terrence threw a wadded up piece of paper at Yannick.

I had been listening to Mr. Tavers since he told us to form a line at the door. I was one of the only ones who were listening. The others who remained standing still in line beside me were Rowena, Adam, Chelsea, Amy, and Clark. Everyone else was behaving as badly as they usually do.

It usually didn't bother me that most of the class acted like this. I was still able to do my work and I usually didn't suffer any repercussions due to their actions. The only time I was punished when the entire class didn't listen was at the beginning of the year, when Mr. Tavers gave everyone detention because only three people did their homework. I was one of the three people that did their homework, but it didn't matter. That day I went home crying and my dad phoned the school. After that day, I never had to experience detention again.

Today was another day where I was being punished for the actions of everyone else. We were supposed to leave at 11:00 AM to go to the museum. It was now almost 11:30 AM, and it didn't seem like we were any closer to leaving. I really hated my classmates, and today that hatred was intensified.

"Listen up everyone. I want everyone to form a line in front of the door right now. If you don't start listening, we'll spend the day in detention instead of going to the museum. That means no recess," Mr. Tavers said.

I followed Chelsea and Amy to the door, and stood behind them. A few more classmates had joined us, but they weren't standing still in line. After a while, Mr. Tavers managed to get everyone to stand still, but it came at a cost. He promised us that if the entire class listened to him from now until we returned from the museum, he wouldn't give us any homework tonight. I was a bit disappointed; I had already completed the homework assignment.

"Listen up. Everyone will walk with a buddy.

You and your buddy have to hold hands at all times. We are going to go outside and walk to the subway station. I expect all of you to be on your best behaviour," Mr. Tavers said to us, as most of my classmates struggled to stay still.

I didn't understand why it was so hard for everyone to listen. It wasn't fair that Mr. Tavers had to go through this. It wasn't fair that any of our teachers over the years have had to go through this. I couldn't wait until graduation. I would finally be in secondary school. My brother David was in secondary school right now, and he said it was much better than elementary school. I couldn't wait until I left this place. Hopefully, I wouldn't have the same classmates I have right now.

I was lost in my train of thought when I noticed Amy was no longer standing in front of me. Quickly snapping out of my daze, I noticed that some of my classmates were standing in the hallway holding hands. I looked to my left and saw Mr. Tavers staring down at me.

"Justin, who's your buddy?" he asked me.

I quickly looked over my shoulder at my classmates, but knew that there was no point. It wasn't like anyone would volunteer to be my buddy.

No one ever did.

Looking down at my feet, I mumbled, "I don't have a buddy."

"Who doesn't have a buddy?" Mr. Tavers asked the class. As he spoke, I tried to make myself as small as possible.

When no one responded, a small wave of relief washed over me. If everyone already had a buddy, maybe I would be allowed to be by myself. I really enjoyed being by myself. But as soon as the thought crossed my mind, it immediately vanished. There was no way I would be able to be by myself. We were twenty-four students in the class, and no one was absent today.

"Does everyone have a buddy?" Mr. Tavers asked again. "Clark? Terrence? Abigail? Naomi?"

As he called Clark's name, the dark cloud that was weighing down on me waned for a moment. I liked Clark. He wasn't really my friends—I didn't have any friends—but he was always nice to me. It would be okay if Clark was my buddy.

"I'm buddies with Elizabeth," Clark answered. The three others he asked responded the same way.

"Don't worry, Justin. You'll have a partner. Everyone's here today, so there's at least one person who also doesn't have a partner. Stand here with me. I'm going to send out all the pairs into to the hallway. Once I'm done, we will have found your buddy," Mr. Tavers said.

I went to go stand beside him, and watched as he called out and ushered students into the hallway, all in groups of two and holding hands. When Greg was at the front of the line, no one was with him.

"Who's your buddy, Greg?" Mr. Tavers asked him.

"I don't know," he replied.

"Justin doesn't have a buddy either. You two can group together. Grab each other's hands and go to the end of the line in the hallway," Mr. Tavers said.

I knew what was going to happen before it even took place, but it still hurt nonetheless. I wished I could just force the ground to crack open and swallow me whole.

"Ew, gross. I'm not going to touch his hand," Greg said, as he glared at me. Turning his back to us, he faced the classroom and shouted: "Who wants to be my buddy? He's trying to force me to be buddies with gross Justin!"

"Watch it, Greg," Mr. Tavers said.

I tried to focus my eyes anywhere but on Greg

and my classmates. I heard someone running towards us, and then a girl's voice, Emma's voice. I liked Emma; she used to be my friend. I missed her. We lived on the same street, and used to play together all the time. One day, she just didn't want to play with me. I didn't even know why she didn't like me anymore.

"Don't worry, Greg. I'll be your buddy so you don't have to touch gross Justin's hands," Emma said. Her words cut through me like sharp splintered glass. I wanted to cry, but I forced myself to hold back my tears.

"I'm warning you two: If I hear either of you say anything else mean about Justin, you're going to the principal's office and not coming with us to the museum. Am I making myself clear?" Mr. Tavers said. I knew he was trying to help, but he would only make things worse.

I watched from the corner of my eye as Greg and Emma went into the hallway and joined the line. I was really excited to go to the museum, but now I wished that I had stayed home. Maybe Mr. Tavers would be upset at the entire class, and cancel the trip. Everyone had quieted down for a while, but they were slowly starting to go back to the way they were before. I closed my eyes and prayed that the trip would be cancelled.

"Okay then, it's just you two left. Come on, partner up," Mr. Tavers said.

I hadn't been paying attention, so I didn't notice that everyone in the classroom was lined up in the hallway except for Mr. Tavers, myself, and Jacob. At that point, I wished Greg had been forced to be my partner. That would have been better than being paired off with Jacob.

"Come on, now. Hold hands and go line up," Mr. Tavers repeated. Jacob grabbed my hand in his pudgy palm and grasped tightly. He was hurting me, but I didn't dare say anything. I followed him out into the hallway, and we stood at the end of the line.

"Everyone, listen up. We're going to go outside and walk to the subway station. Do not let go of your buddy's hands. Make sure that you stay in line and follow your classmates in front of you. Is all of that clear? Yes? Alright then, let's go," Mr. Tavers said, as he led us through the hallway through the front doors of the school.

While we were walking, Jacob kept on squeezing my hand. I felt like he was breaking my hand, but I didn't say anything or make a sound. If I did, it would just make things worse. After a few minutes, he gave up. Instead of squeezing my hand, he started kicking me from behind. When he would kick me, I had to concentrate so I wouldn't fall down. My leg was hurting, and I already knew it was bruised without actually having to look at it. Regardless, I continued walking with my hand stuck in the grips of Jacob's hand.

As we approached the subway station, a small wave of relief washed over me. At least Mr. Tavers would be able to watch all of us while we're sitting in the subway. Jacob wouldn't dare hurt me in front of Mr. Tavers.

While we waited for Mr. Tavers to pay our fare, I felt something hit me in the head. At first I ignored it, but then I felt something else hit me again. I turned around to catch Emma and Greg throwing small pebbles in my direction. When they noticed me watching, they started laughing and continued throwing them at me.

I turned back around and focused my attention on Mr. Tavers. He was done paying our fare, and opened a gate to let us all through. I tried to walk a little faster so that we would be walking close to Mr. Tavers, but Jacob caught on, squeezed my hand, and slowed our pace until we were once again at the back of the group.

When we reached the subway platform, we were made to stand with our backs against the wall. Mr. Tavers was just finishing counting us to make sure we were all there, when the subway arrived. As it pulled into the station, Jacob took the opportunity to head-butt me. The sound of the train masked the sound of our heads colliding. Holding a hand to my head, I forced myself to remain quiet, even though I felt like screaming until my lungs were empty.

As the subway doors opened, we walked into the train. There were only a few people in the train, so it looked like there would be enough seats for everyone to sit down. I tried to maneuver towards two empty seats, but Jacob pulled me back. Instead, he made his way towards Terrence and Lee. They were sitting in a section that had three seats. Jacob took the third seat, and forced me to stand for the entire trip.

Royal York

I held onto my daughter Annabella as tightly as I could manage. She was slung across my body, resting her sleeping head on my shoulder. Every step I took made my body wince in pain, but I couldn't stop now. I didn't know where I was headed, but knew that it was far away from here.

After walking for about half an hour, I couldn't support her weight anymore. It wasn't safe to stop in the streets, so I looked around and focused on my surroundings for the first time since I set foot outside my door. I spotted a fast food restaurant, and made my way inside.

Once inside, I headed to the seating area on the far right side, which was shielded from the staff. I set Annabella down on a seat, as I gently coaxed her awake.

"Sweetie? Wake up, sweetie," I whispered to her, as her eyes gently rolled open.

"Where are we, mommy?" she asked me.

Fighting back tears, I managed to push a smile to the forefront. "We're at a restaurant, sweetie. Are you hungry? Tell mommy what you want to eat."

She shook her head from side to side, and started banging her hands against the table. I didn't want to draw any attention to us. I slung off my bag that was hung across my back, and brought it to rest in my lap. Fishing my hand inside, I felt around until my hands found my phone.

"Do you want to play your game?" I asked her, as I unlocked my phone and navigated to her favorite game. She immediately stopped banging the table and reached out for the phone. I eagerly handed it to her, happy that she was now occupied.

Focusing my attention back to the matter at hand, I tried to think quickly. What should I do? Where should I go? I had managed to bring my wallet with me, but I only had a little bit of cash. I didn't want to risk using any of my debit or credit cards. He was probably checking the activity online right now, trying to figure out where I fled to.

I looked at Annabella playing with my phone, and a surge of courage swept through me. There was a reason I left. I couldn't leave Annabella there. I couldn't let her grow up witnessing what went on in that home. No, it wasn't a home. A home is somewhere you belong.

Wiping the corners of my eyes discreetly so

that she wouldn't notice, I took a ten dollar bill from my wallet before placing it in my bag. As I zipped up the closure, I noticed that there was a tear in it. It must have happened as we were leaving; I hadn't even noticed.

"Annabella, sweetie, can you stay here while mommy goes to buy us something to eat?" I asked her. She was focused on her game, and didn't remove her eyes from the screen. I took her nodding her head as acceptance, and made my way to the order counter.

"Hi, how can I help you?" I was greeted by a perky teenager, who was sporting a wide smile on their face.

"Hi. Can I please get a small fry, two small burgers, and a small soda, please?" I ordered. I had mentally calculated the total prior to ordering, and was sure that the $10 I had would cover it.

"Is that everything?" he asked me.

"Yes, thank you," I replied.

"That will be $6.29," he said. His smile never left his face.

I handed him my money and took the change that he handed back. Pocketing the change, I grabbed the cup he had placed on the counter and went to go fill it up with soda. Standing in front of the soda dispenser, I gulped down half of the contents. Wiping my mouth with the corner of my sleeve, I refilled the soda I just drank.

By the time I went back to the counter, my order was already finished. I grabbed the tray, placing my soda on it, and made my way back to Annabella. Setting the tray down on the table, I opened up the wrapper for her burger, and spread some fries beside it.

Grabbing my phone back from her, I guided her to her food. She protested at first, but it didn't take long for her to dig into her food. I guess she was hungrier than she thought. After watching her chew her first few bites, I removed the wrapper from my own burger and brought it to my mouth. As I took my first bite, I realized just how hungry I had been. One burger would not be enough.

I finished my burger and half of the fries, before Annabella had even finished eating half of hers. I remained motionless, watching her eat. It was comforting, and safe. The imagery of just watching her take a small bite of her burger, and chew made me feel like everything was normal. But it wasn't normal. It was never normal.

As she continued eating, I grabbed my phone and mentally prepared myself. I couldn't avoid this forever. There was no other choice; I had no one else to turn to. Unlocking my phone, I navigated through my contacts until I came upon my sister's number. Dialing her number, I pressed the phone up to my ears.

As the phone rang, the loudness of the ring accelerated my heart beat. I caught myself holding my breath during every silent moment in between the rings, in anticipation of the phone being answered. After the fourth ring, my sister picked up.

"Hello?" she greeted. Her voice was full of life and happiness. I couldn't do this to her. I couldn't bring her into this. It wouldn't be fair to her. However, I had no other choice.

"Hello? Jennifer? I know it's you, I have caller ID," she said, after I had failed to acknowledge her greeting. I was stuck in my mind, and hadn't even noticed that I failed to respond to her.

"Oh, sorry. Hi Sarah. How are you?" I asked her.

"I'm fine. How are you, Jennifer? You don't sound okay. Did something happen to Annabella?" she asked.

In spite of my mentally exhausting attempts at shielding the pain from my voice, I had failed. She always knew when there was something wrong. I couldn't hide this from her. She would want to help; I needed to remember that. She was my sister; she was always there for me.

"I...," my words trailed off, as I tried to bring myself to speak. Why was it so hard to say it? Probably because then I would have to accept it, once I said it out loud.

As I focused on regaining my composure to address my sister, I noticed Annabella staring at me. She had stopped eating and was looking at me with concern in her eyes. Seeing that look in her eyes gave me all the courage I needed. I had to be there for her, I had to be strong.

"Eat, Annabella. Come on, eat. Mommy's just talking to Auntie Sarah," I whispered to her, as I forced a smile to spread across my lips. She looked at me for a few seconds, before going back to her food.

"Jennifer, what's going on?" Sarah asked. There was a hint of panic in her voice, although I knew she was doing her best to hide it.

"I'm sorry, Sarah. I called you because..." I couldn't finish my sentence, so I tried again. "I left."

As those two words escaped my lips, I let out a sigh.

"Did he touch you? Did he touch Annabella?" she asked. Her tone was very forceful. I knew that she was being protective, but it didn't matter. Before I even realized what was happening, tears started coursing down my face.

"Listen to me, okay. Listen to me, Jennifer. You need to come to my house. We'll figure all of this out, but you need to be safe. Where are you?" she asked.

Wiping my eyes and nose with the back of my sleeve, I told her where we were.

"Okay. I'm going to leave work right now and come pick you up," she said.

I didn't want her to do that. I didn't want her to have to drive all the way across town and waste her time and gas in traffic. I also didn't want to stay here until she came. Just in case.

"No, no. Sarah, it's okay. I can take the subway. I have tokens, so I'm okay," I replied.

"No, I'm not going to let you take the subway. I'll come and get you. I'm leaving work right now." She wouldn't relent. She was my sister; she wanted to protect me, the same way I wanted to protect Annabella.

"Please, Sarah. It will be faster if I take the subway. I don't want to stay her any longer than I have too," I pleaded with her.

There was silence on the other end of the line, until she finally answered: "Okay. Just promise me you'll be safe. That bastard. That damn bastard! I swear, I'm going to kill him! I'm going to—"

"Please," I interrupted her. "Please, not now."

"I'm sorry," she replied. Her tone had calmed. My heart rate started to slow down a bit. It would be okay. Everything would be okay.

"I'm going to leave work right now, and I'm headed straight home. Call me when you get to the subway station, and I'll come pick you up. I don't want you walking all that distance by yourself," she said.

"Okay. Thank you, Sarah. Thank you," I said.

As I hung up the phone, I noticed Annabella had been observing me for a while. Her head was cocked to the side, and there was a questioning look in her eyes.

"Mommy?" she asked.

"Yes, sweetie," I answered, cupping her cheek in the palm of my hand.

"Are you crying because daddy hurt you?" she

asked me.

I could feel a new wave of tears fighting to burst through, but I had to keep them back. I had to keep them back for her. Swallowing the little saliva that was in my mouth, I told her: "Yes."

I expected her to follow up with a bunch of questions, but her response surprised me. I watched as she gathered all of the garbage on the table and threw it out. When she came back, she walked over to me and reached for my hands.

"Mommy, I'll take care of you. I'll help you get better," she said. She stood on the tips of her toes, and gave me a kiss on my forehead. I couldn't keep the tears at bay anymore, and they started flooding down my face. I grabbed her in a hug, and held her tightly.

Grabbing my bag, we made our way outside of the restaurant. I held her hand as we walked towards the subway station. I kept on glancing behind my back every once in a while, but there was no sign of him.

When we arrived at the subway station, I paid our fare and we made our way to the platform. I watched as the subway pulled into the station, until it came to a standstill in front of us. Still holding onto

Annabella's hand, we made our way into the train. As we sat down, I rested my head against the window and closed my eyes. Before the train had a chance to pull out of the station, Annabella was tugging at my sleeve.

"Mommy, can I play my game?" she asked.

"Of course, sweetie. Just be careful," I said, as I retrieved my phone from my bag and set up the game for her.

Old Mill

Lacing up my skates, I gave them a final tug before returning my full weight to my knees. Taking a deep breath, I pushed off from the ground with my fists, transferring my momentum to my legs. Slowly, but steadily, I managed to rise to a standing position.

A smile spread across my face, as my legs started shaking and fighting for balance. Pain was shooting through my lower legs, up into my lower back. It didn't matter; none of it mattered. All that mattered was that I had successfully managed to stand up on my skates without falling down.

Taking in a few deep controlled breaths, I reached out for the arm of my couch. Focusing all my concentration on the task at hand, I rolled one leg forward and mimicked the same motion with my other leg. As hard as all of this was, it was worth it for me.

Exhausted, I maneuvered myself until the couch was behind me. Unceremoniously, I plopped down and allowed the overstuffed cushions to soften my fall. I unlaced my skates and slipped them off my feet. I remained seated on the couch, reclining my head all the way back until I was face to face with the ceiling.

"Are you all set?" Kailey, my roommate, called to me from the bathroom. She had just finished taking a shower and the steam that was trapped inside was released as she opened the door.

"Just about," I replied back.

Getting up from the couch, I grabbed my skates and placed them into my duffel bag. I had purchased a new duffel bag specifically for this occasion. Although it was rather large and bulky, it had a wheeled pulley system, which it made it really easy to tug around. I checked my bag to make sure everything I needed was packed: roller skates, helmet, elbow pads, knee pads, wrist guards, mouth guard, socks, deodorant, and $50 cash. Satisfied with the contents, I zipped up the bag and placed it near the front of the apartment door.

Kailey was still in the bathroom getting ready. She usually required an unexplainable amount of time to get ready each morning. It didn't bother me, but that was most likely due to the fact that she would always allow me to have first dibs on the bathroom if we needed it at the same time.

Knocking gingerly on the open bathroom

door, I waited until she acknowledged me before walking behind her into the bathroom. I wasn't too keen on sneaking up on her, especially when she was wielding a hot curling iron.

"Are you sure you don't mind going with me?" I asked her, taking a seat on the side of the bathtub.

"Of course I don't mind, Pam. I already told you I would go to support you. Plus, I don't really know what roller derby is. Maybe I'll learn something while I'm there," she responded.

I feigned mock shock on my face. "What do you mean you don't know what roller derby is? I've been talking about it non-stop for the last four months. The first time I went to a game was with you and Fraz, when he won tickets from the radio station. Clearly, you weren't paying attention."

"Yeah, so sue me," she said, a hint of laughter escaping her lips.

"Are you going to be ready in fifteen minutes?" I asked her, as I got up and started making my way out of the bathroom.

"Probably not, but I'll try," she responded.

"You have fifteen minutes. You promised. Get to it," I said, as I left the bathroom.

Making my way back to the living room, I sat

back down on the couch. I had to keep myself happy and occupied, or else I would start doubting myself. I would start doubting that I would actually be able to learn how to skate in just a few months' time. I would start doubting that I would actually be selected to train as Fresh Meat, the designation giving to all new initiates of roller derby.

The first time I was ever made aware of the existence of roller derby was when Kailey's boyfriend Fraz had brought us to a game, after winning tickets on a radio show. I had only tagged along for the company on a Saturday evening, since I had never heard of the sport before. After seeing that first game, I had been enthralled ever since. Since my first introduction to the sport, I hadn't missed a single game. One night after perusing the team's website, I noticed an ad for their next round of Fresh Meat. They were inviting all those who were interested in pursuing the sport to try out for a spot in the program. Not only would the program teach you all the basics of roller derby from the ground up, but it was also formulated in such a way that no previous skating experience was required. Considering the fact that the last time I had laced up a pair of skates was at a Grade 5 field trip, I surely needed the instruction.

Once accepted into the Fresh Meat program, you would train for months on end until you became proficient. If you were able to pass all the basic qualifications, you got accepted into the league. After that, there's a drafting period where teams select new players to add to their rosters from the successful pool of Fresh Meat candidates. More than anything, that's what I wanted.

Even though today was the first day I had managed to stand up on my skates without falling over, I wasn't afraid. No, that was I lie. I was afraid, but I knew deep down that there was no reason to be afraid. They would teach me to skate, and the rest would grow from there.

"Ready?" Kailey asked, as she slung her purse over her shoulder.

"I hope so," I replied, as I got up from the couch. I followed Kailey to the front door and grabbed the handle from my duffel bag as we headed out.

The air outside was fresh and crisp. I allowed my mind and body to relax as we made our way to the subway station. Fraz had offered to give us a ride in his car, but he got called into work at the last minute. However, I didn't mind. Taking public transit might just afford me enough time to calm down my nerves.

We both walked in silence until we reached the subway station. Kailey went through the turnstiles with her monthly pass, but I had to wait in line to buy tokens. As soon as I had my tokens in hand, I dropped one into the receptacle and pushed my weight against the turnstile.

"Do you want me to grab your bag?" Kailey asked, motioning for my bag with her hand.

I shook my head. "No, it's okay. It's not that heavy anyway; I'm just pulling it along. Thanks anyway," I replied.

Once we found ourselves on the platform, my heart started pounding against my chest. I couldn't wait to lace up my skates and join the other Fresh Meat initiates. At the same time, I was scared to death of being the worst skater there. I couldn't wait to put all of my effort into the training for the next coming months, successfully passing the basic qualifications test. At the same time, I was scared to death of failing miserably. Or worse yet, of being the only one who had difficulties grasping the basics.

As we waited for the train to arrive, I closed my eyes. I took a deep breath in, and another deep breath out. I felt the blood coursing through my veins, the rise and fall of my chest above my frenzied heart. As I took in another deep breath, I heard the sound of an approaching train. Before I could open my eyes, I felt a gust of wind being blown in my face. Opening my eyes, I looked at Kailey as we waited for the train doors to open.

"You've got this," she said, squeezing my left shoulder. A smile spread on her face, as she tried to replace the one I hadn't realized I had lost.

A smile slowly spread across my lips, the tops corners extending as far north as they could. The smile grew to such heights, that a small hint of nervous laughter escaped my lips. Nervous or not, I knew what I wanted. What I wanted was to play roller derby. In order to achieve that goal, this was the first step I had to take. There were no shortcuts or easy ways out. Achieving my goal would require a lot of hard work, but the difficulty of the work was nothing compared the drive that burned within the depths of my being.

"I've got this," I said to Kailey, as the subway doors opened.

Walking into the subway, I made a beeline for two free seats. Yes, roller derby would require a lot of hard work. But that work wouldn't begin until I laced my skates up later today. For now, I rested my head against the window, daydreaming of skating with grace, elegance, and voracity on the track.

Jane

I placed a stack of folded shirts into my suitcase, right beside a neatly folded stack of pants. Holding my hand in between the gap formed by the two piles, I crammed as many pairs of socks into it as I could. Unzipping the upper compartment inside my suitcase, I placed my bras and underwear inside. As I closed my suitcase shut, all hopes I had of consolidating suitcases with my fiancé were dashed.

"Brock, can you come here for a second?" I called out to my fiancé.

I heard the pitter-patter of light feet, before I finally heard his heavy footfalls ascend the staircase. I craned my neck to the side, just in time to see my son Keen walk into the room. Brock followed behind shortly, scooping him up into his arms and he entered the room.

"Are you almost done packing?" he asked, as he squeezed Keen tightly in his arms.

"Just about," I replied. "I still need to pack Keen's stuff. I didn't have enough room to fit anything in mine. Do you think you could squeeze his clothes into yours?"

I watched as Brock dropped Keen on the bed, and walked over to the closet. He pulled out a suitcase, and placed in on the bed. As he unzipped it, I silently prayed that there would be enough room inside. I didn't expect, however, that his suitcase would be empty.

"What the hell, Brock? I thought you said you finished packing all of your things?" I yelled at him, in exasperation.

"Relax, I did pack. Look," he said, as he unzipped the compartment inside the suitcase. I watched as he pulled out a toothbrush, swimming trunks, and a pair of underwear. "You packed toothpaste in your suitcase, right?"

I let out a sigh of frustration, and grabbed Keen into my arms. I walked to his room, and placed him on his bed. I riffled through his bookshelf until I found a comic book, and handed it to him. I didn't even have to tell him anything; he opened it and started reading it as soon as it was in his hands. Returning to my bedroom, I composed myself in anticipation of facing off with Brock.

"What the hell kind of packing is that?" I silently yelled at him, as I slammed the door behind me. I picked up the items he had taken out, and slammed them back into his suitcase. "We're going away and this is how you pack?"

"Relax. We're only going to be gone for two days," he replied.

I couldn't believe it. I had tasked him with the easiest chore in the world, and he couldn't even do that properly. We had less than half an hour before we had to leave, and I couldn't even count on him to help me.

I went over to our dresser and opened his drawers. I pulled out two pairs of pants, two t-shirts, two pairs of boxers, socks, a pair of underwear, and a belt. As I walked towards the closest, I made a pit stop in front of the bed and dumped everything I was holding inside.

I angrily tore off one of his button-down shirts from the hanger it was hanging on in the closet, and threw it into the suitcase. Not even bothering to look at him, I quickly ran to Keen's room and piled up his clothes. When I returned to the room, Brock was sporting a smile. I wanted to rip it off his smug face.

"Why don't you chill? We're only going to be gone for two days. I'm just going to wear what I'm wearing right now. It's not a big deal. It's not hot, so I won't sweat," he said.

I ignored him as I continued packing his suitcase. I had managed to fit all of his clothing, along with Keen's, inside of the suitcase. Pressing the top down and applying pressure with my hand, I zipped up the suitcase.

"See? Was that so hard? God! Why did I marry an idiot?" I spat at him.

He was still sporting that ridiculous smile on his face. "We're not married yet."

"Yeah. If you keep this up, we won't ever get married," I replied.

I lined up both suitcases in front of the door, and tried to remember if I was forgetting anything. He was still standing in the same position. His arms were crossed against his body, and he was still sporting that stupid smile.

"Can you just stop it? Stop smiling! What the hell is wrong with you?" I shouted at him. I kicked his suitcase, and it fell over with a thud.

"Okay, you need to calm down. Why are you being so psychotic?" he asked. The smile had now disappeared from his smug face. Good.

I ignored him, and walked out of the room. As I was passing through the hallway, I checked in on Keen. He was still reading his comic book. I closed his door, and went downstairs. I could hear Brock following behind me.

"Can you stop for a second and talk to me? What's going on? Why are you acting like this?" he asked.

Still ignoring him, I continued walking into the kitchen. I was so upset, that I didn't even know what I was doing. I had to continue moving, or else... At this point, I did not know what I was capable of. I surely did not want to test it before we left for our first vacation together.

"Can you just talk to me? What's going on? Why are you so angry?" he asked again. He was now in the kitchen with me, at the other end of the counter.

I slowly turned around and faced him. "You want to know what's wrong? You really want to know what's wrong? How about the fact that you're too stupid to pack up a suitcase. I mean, how difficult is it? You get your clothes, you put it in your suitcase, and you zip it up. It's not rocket science. You're such a retard," I said to him. I was so angry that I was spitting on him as I was talking.

"Hey," he replied. He didn't raise his voice; he was still talking calmly. "I told you to stop using that word. It's really offensive, you know. The way you're using it, it's not right."

In that moment, I knew exactly how to get him. I knew how to break him, and that was exactly what I was going to do. Looking him straight in the eyes, I snapped: "Why? Oh, yeah. I forgot your cousin Malcolm's a retard. It must run in the family."

I could see the rage build inside of him. I had succeeded; I had struck one of the only nerves in his better-than-thou mind. I was itching for him to react. One hit. One hit would be all it would take, and then I could take him for all he had.

I watched as he stared at me. I could tell he was angry, but he wasn't saying anything. He was standing still, breathing heavily. I was silently goading him on with my eyes, just daring him to hit me. After a few minutes of silence, he finally spoke.

"I'm not doing this with you. I'm not going to stoop to your level. I'm not going to fight with you," he said calmly.

I watched as he turned around, without saying another word. What was wrong with him? He was walking towards the stairs, and I followed closely behind him.

"Where do you think you're going? Where are

you going?" I shouted at him, demanding answers for his rude behaviour.

Ignoring me, I watched as he opened the door to Keen's room. He picked him up, and headed into our bedroom. He squatted down to retrieve his suitcase that I had kicked over, and turned back around to face me.

"I'm going to my parents' house. I'll be back before you get back from vacation. Maybe that'll give you enough time to cool off," he said.

As the words came flowing out of his mouth, I couldn't believe what I was hearing. How dare he? Who did he think he was? Keen wasn't even his biological child.

"Are you okay, buddy?" I heard him ask Keen.

Keen nodded his head. "Where are we going, daddy?"

That sent me over the top. I couldn't contain myself anymore. "He's not your daddy! Your daddy didn't want you!" As soon as the words came out of my mouth, I clasped my hands to my chest. I didn't mean to say that to Keen. My poor Keen.

"We're going on a little vacation, buddy," Brock replied to Keen, kissing his forehead lightly.

With Keen in tow, Brock headed down the

stairs and towards the front door. He placed Keen on the floor, and reached for his jacket that was hanging near the door. I watched as he put on Keen's jacket, and firmly held onto his hand. His other hand was on the door knob. I watched silently, unable to react.

"Please call me once you get there. Enjoy those two days, and just try to enjoy yourself. I know you're stressed. This is the best thing for all of us. As I said, I'll be home before you come back, and hopefully we'll be able to enjoy my last day of vacation together, before I go back to work," he said.

I remained silent, unable to say anything in response. He looked at me for a few seconds, before opening the door. Grabbing his suitcase, he stepped into the doorframe of the door. "Thanks for packing my suitcase. I love you. Please, just try to relax."

Motionless, I watched as he disappeared from view. The front door closed, and the house was silent. Sobbing, I went to retrieve my suitcase in my room. Grabbing my purse from the kitchen, I headed to the door and left. I was hoping that they were still outside, but they were gone. Controlling my emotions, I set my face to neutral and started walking towards the subway station.

Once I arrived at the subway station, I angrily

slammed my token into the receptacle. Pulling my suitcase behind me, I made my way to the subway platform. Waiting for the train, I ran through the recent course of events through my mind.

As the train pulled into the station, I held my head up high. Good riddance. It's better this way. Now I'll actually be able to enjoy my vacation, without having to put up with Keen or Brock. As the subway doors slid open, I walked in with a wide grin spread across my face.

Runnymede

Everyone thought that I was crazy, but that was alright with me. I may have been wrong this time, but they'll be kissing my feet when my hunch proves correct. It's just a matter of time before I finally figure out the formula, and then I'll be able to spot them all.

I was walking on the sidewalk, still wearing my work uniform. I had been at work for little more than two hours and a half, when my supervisor approached me. Standing staunchly with one hand on his hips, he stared boldly into my eyes.

"I hope you realize that what you did was wrong, and I'm not dealing with a complete moron," he had said. Spit flew onto my face as he spoke.

"They are everywhere. They are hiding amongst us," I replied, as I passed a dirty rag over the counter, cleaning up a coffee spill.

"You know I'm going to have to fire you, right? Christ, you couldn't even make it one month. I tried giving you a chance, but I can't allow you to stay after what you did," he replied.

"Thank you," I told him, as I folded the rag

and placed it in the center of the counter. "You will be happy to know that you are safe. Everyone here is human. I think."

"Good luck, Carver," he said, exasperated. I could feel him watching me as I made my way out of the restaurant, and disappeared from sight.

As far as I was concerned, I wasn't doing anything wrong. I was providing humanity with a service. For the past six years, I have been working on a formula to determine if there's an alien presence inside a human body. I still have yet to perfect it, but I was getting close.

Approximately eight years ago, I was visited by Aeborgh. He told me he was from the planet Asjn, and that he had an important message to deliver. Warriors from his planet were sent on a mission to infiltrate Earth by hijacking human bodies. He indicated that their ultimate plan was to overtake the planet, and claim it as their own. Their sun was dying, and Earth was the closest planet that mimicked their atmosphere.

Aeborgh was exiled from his planet, because he spoke out against the plan. He proposed contacting Earth and reaching an agreement where both species could live peacefully. The governing bodies were vehemently opposed to such a recommendation, and exiled him for treason.

At first I thought I was hallucinating or dreaming. I had just had a couple of drinks at a bar, and thought that someone may have slipped something into my drink. I slowly reached out my hand to touch him, when I felt a strong coil grip across my wrist. It was at that moment that I realized I wasn't dreaming; Aeborgh was real.

He pulled at my wrist until it went numb, and placed his head against mine. I remember thinking how cold and clammy it felt, like cold perspiration. I could feel my heartbeat and hear my breath, as I waited for him to speak.

Only seconds went by, but they felt like hours. I was just hoping that he wouldn't kill me. I didn't know what he wanted with me. I silently prayed that I wouldn't end up as his snack.

When he finally let go of my wrist, he told me that he would be back with instructions on how to build a detector. I wasn't too sure what he was talking about, and I didn't really care. After he continued staring at me for a few more seconds, he left.

For two years, I had lived in peace, looking back on the memory as a distorted dream. It couldn't have been real. There was no way that an alien had come into my home, had touched me, and had spoken to me. I finally managed to put the entire ordeal to the back of my mind, when he reappeared.

This time, Aeborgh seemed much gentler than before. It could be that I was the first human he contacted, and he hadn't known how to act back then. Or it could just be that I was so scared last time, that I hadn't had the chance to register anything but fear.

Reaching for my right arm, he pulled until my arm was perpendicular to the floor. Grasping my hand, he covered it with his. I felt something heavy drop into my hand. As he removed his hand, I quickly closed my hand so that the object wouldn't drop. Bringing my hand back down, I glanced into my palm. There was a small orb-like object sitting it the palm of my hand. Although it was black, it also appeared transparent.

"What is this?" I asked him.

He started speaking in a language I did not understand. I couldn't tell what it was, but it sounded like Chinese. I didn't know a single word in Chinese, but I remembered what watching Chinese martial arts movies sounded like.

When he stopped talking, I assumed that he

realized I wasn't able to understand him. He craned his head to the left, and I heard a small crack. Suddenly, he started speaking to me in English.

"Use this pharh to call me, when you've found an Asjn warrior. Simply swallow it into your body. The acids within you will activate the pharh," he said.

"What? How do I even know if there's a…" I paused, unable to pronounce the name of his planet. "How do I know there's one of them in one of us?"

"You hold the answers within yourself," he said.

I didn't understand what he was telling me, nor was I absolutely sure that I wasn't dreaming up the entire ordeal. As I opened my mouth to ask him for clarification, he disappeared.

Ever since that day, I have been hard at work trying to figure out the formula to detect an alien in a human body. I was almost positive that I had the correct formula, but I still needed to find a human body inhabited by an alien to test it out.

As I continued walking, I stuck my hands into my pockets. I felt the syringe and vial containers in my pocket. I still had seven vials left, after testing everyone I worked with. Well, almost everyone. I was unable to test my supervisor and one cashier. I was fired before I had the chance.

I spotted a small convenience store, and made my way towards it. As I opened the door, the little bell on top of it chimed. I was greeted by a sullen teenager, who immediately turned back to his magazine after spotting me. At first I dismissed him, but thoughts started forming in my mind. Wouldn't that be a good vessel to use? A young body, with the freedom to do what most adults could not without attracting too must scrutiny.

I walked towards the fridge, and opened the door. The sudden flash of cold felt good against my skin. Ever since our first encounter, the cold comforted me. Grabbing a bottle of soda, I made my way towards the counter.

"$2.25," the sullen teenager said, not even looking at me.

Sticking my hand into my pocket, I carefully affixed a vial to the syringe. Still staring at him, I could tell that he would most likely not look my way. This was the perfect opportunity. Pulling the syringe out of my pocket, I quickly jabbed it into his hand and forced all of the contents from the vial inside.

"What the hell, man!" he yelled, as he pulled his hand away. I continued staring at his hand, waiting for it to change colours. It didn't.

I wasn't paying attention, so I didn't realize I was being swung at until I felt something hard hit the side of my head. Falling backwards onto the ground, the syringe fell from my hand. I dragged my hand across the floor looking for it. As I found it and tried to grasp it into my hand, I felt something hard hit me in the stomach.

Looking up, I saw the teenager standing over me. He had come out from behind the counter, and looked furious. He was about to launch another kick into my midsection, but I quickly rolled out of the way. Spotting the syringe I had failed to grasp before, I picked it up and shoved it quickly into my pocket.

Getting up to my feet, I ran towards the door. I felt something hit my back right before the door closed behind me, but I was okay. I continued running until I was well out of sight from the store. The teenager hadn't followed me outside the store as far as I could tell, but I didn't want to take any chances. This was a very dangerous job.

I spotted a park bench and slowed my pace. Sinking down into the bench, I retrieved my notebook from my pocket. Turning to the middle of the book, I stared at the formula I had written down.

Maybe this formula was wrong. If it was, I would have to start all over again. I would have to retest everyone that previously passed the test.

Having sufficiently gathered my breath, I got up and continued walking. I was going to head to the library, but decided against it. It would be best if I headed home, and worked on the formula some more. I only had to walk for a few minutes, before I spotted the sign for the subway.

Heading into the subway station, I paid my fare and made my way to the platform. There were six other people also waiting for the subway with me. I still had enough vials to test everyone here, but it would be too risky. They would be tested in time, but not today.

As the subway pulled into the station, I walked inside. Looking around, I counted only three others in the train. Three was a manageable number. Sticking my hand into my pocket, I manoeuvered the used vial off of the syringe and affixed a new one to it.

High Park

"Andrew, aren't you forgetting something?" my mom called out to me, as I made a dash for the door. Turning around, I ran back into the kitchen and gave her a quick kiss on the cheek.

"I love you, mom," I said, turning around and running back towards the door. "I'll be back before ten!"

Opening the door, I ran out onto the porch and listened as the door automatically shut behind me. I knew it hadn't shut all the way, but my mom would close it for me. I continued running until I reached the sidewalk, and continued my pace all the way to the end of the street.

By the time I arrived at Thomas's house, I was panting. Slouched over with my hands over my knees, I took in a few deep breaths. I was looking down at the pavement, so I didn't realize that there was someone standing in front of me.

"What are you doing here?" I heard someone say above me. The voice was huskier than Thomas's; I had never heard it before.

Standing up, I studied the boy standing in

front of me. I recognized him from school. He was a lot bigger than I was, and his face always looked angry.

"Hi Sean," I said.

He took a step towards me, causing me to step backwards. I tripped over my own feet, but caught myself before I fell.

"I said, what are you doing here?" he said, leaning his face directly into mine.

I was too scared to respond. I kept on staring at him, hoping he would leave me alone. I didn't want him to beat me up. His reputation at school was horrible. Up until today, I had avoided his wrath.

"Hi Andrew!" I heard Thomas shouting from behind me. I turned around and saw him running down his porch.

"You know this twerp?" Sean asked Thomas, pointing to me.

"Yes, it's Andrew. He's cool. Leave him alone," Thomas said.

Sean relaxed his demeanor and no longer looked as threatening. I looked from Thomas to Sean, and tried to understand what was going on. Since when did they start hanging out together? We were supposed to play video games all day long, but something told me our plans were about to change.

"Come on, let's go," Sean said. "We're already late."

Thomas started following Sean, so I followed closely behind. I was still scared of Sean, but it didn't seem like he would do anything to me while Thomas was around. As we continued walking, I tried leaning close to Thomas so that Sean wouldn't notice.

"Hey, Thomas. Where are we going?" I asked him in a whisper. I quickly looked ahead at Sean to make sure he didn't hear me. He didn't react, so either he didn't hear or he didn't care.

"We're going to the corner store to get some snacks," he replied.

"But I didn't bring any money," I said to him.

Thomas shrugged his shoulders and continued walking. Both of them were walking at a fast pace, and I had to pump my legs as fast as they would go to keep up. By the time they stopped walking, I was panting and out of breath.

"What's wrong with you? You don't know how to walk?" Sean said to me, as he shot me a sneer. He was still intimidating, but I didn't think he would hurt me.

I turned around to look at Thomas, expecting

him to defend me as he had in front of his house. He laughed nervously and broke eye contact with me. Why was he acting like this?

"Come on, let's go. What do you guys want to get?" Sean asked.

"Let's get some chips and some pop," Thomas replied. "What do you want, Andrew?"

Looking down at my feet, I shrugged my shoulders. "Nothing. I don't have any money."

"Neither do we," Sean replied.

I watched as Sean and Thomas walked into the store. I stayed where I was, staring at the door. How were they going to buy anything if they didn't have money? There were rumours at school that Sean stole things from stores. Were they going to steal? Why would Thomas do something like that?

I nervously shuffled about, shifting all my weight on one foot and then the other. I didn't know what to do. If I left and went home, Thomas might be mad at me. I closed my eyes and took a deep breath.

As I opened my eyes, I saw Sean and Thomas running out of the convenience store. Thomas was holding a bag of chips and a two liter bottle of soda. Sean was holding a handful of chocolate bars and candy, clutched closely to his chest.

"Run, you idiot! Run!" Sean screamed at me, as he ran down the street and disappeared behind a fence.

Thomas was running behind him, although not as fast. I didn't know what to do, so I just followed him. As I began running, I heard the door to the convenience store open.

"Hey you! You stupid kids! I'm going to call the police!" a man called out from the store.

Scared out of my mind, I pumped my legs harder and harder, running faster than I ever had before. After a while, I couldn't hear the man yelling anymore. I didn't hear any police sirens, so I was hopeful that the police wouldn't catch up to us. Even though I hadn't done anything, I knew I would be punished along with Sean and Thomas.

Sean ran behind a pharmacy and disappeared from view. Thomas and I continued running after him. After we caught up to him, we saw him sitting down against the pharmacy's back wall, his trove of chocolates and candy spread between his open legs.

I watched as Thomas sat down beside him, dropping the bag of chips and bottle of soda on the floor. Sean opened the bottle of soda and chugged a fourth of the contents in one gulp. He handed the bottle to Thomas when he was done. Thomas tried to mimic him, but he started chocking and sputtering soda everywhere.

"Let's see if you can do any better," Sean said, motioning for me to join them.

I carefully approached them, and sat down beside Thomas. I took the bottle of soda that was handed to me, and tried to chug down as much of it as I could. I was managing to swallow a lot more than I anticipated, but I started chocking and accidentally spit the pop in my mouth back into the bottle.

"Eww, gross. Backwashing noob," Sean said. He grabbed a rock from the floor and threw it at me.

As the rock hit me, I felt a stinging sensation in my arm. The pain was gone as soon as it hit. Thank goodness that he was only able to find a small rock to throw at me. I rubbed my arm to make him think it hurt more than it had, so he wouldn't feel the need to do anything more severe.

"Here, eat up," Sean said. He handed a chocolate bar to Thomas, and then to me.

"Thanks," I said.

"What a loser. 'Thanks'. Yeah, that's really gonna get you far in life," Sean replied.

I unwrapped my chocolate bar as quietly as I

could. Sinking my teeth into the bar, I savoured the taste of chocolate. I hadn't realized how hungry I had been. Thomas's mom usually brought us a bunch of snacks whenever I came over to play, so I usually didn't eat anything at home before leaving.

Keeping my gaze directly ahead, I listened to what Thomas and Sean were talking about. If I stayed quiet and didn't interfere, maybe Sean would leave me alone. That's what I was hoping for.

"So, what do you want to do?" Thomas asked Sean.

"I don't know. Why don't you ask the noob what he wants to do?" he replied.

Hearing then refer to me, I slowly turned and focused my gaze on Sean. "We could go play video games at Thomas's house. His mom just bought him the new—"

"Hey, do you have that new shooter game that just came out?" Sean interrupted, turning his attention to Thomas.

"No, my mom doesn't let me play those games," he replied.

I watched as Sean got up, stuffing as many chocolate and candy bars into his pockets as possible. He took the bottle of soda and threw it as far as he

67

could. As the bottle hit the pavement, the impact caused the soda to spray everywhere.

"Come, let's go," Sean said.

Thomas got up and started following Sean. He didn't ask him where we were headed, and I didn't want to ask. I kept as far away from Sean as possible, without seeming as if I were afraid of him.

We walked for a while, before we finally stopped in front of the entrance of a subway station. I was silently praying that Sean wasn't going to make us take the subway.

"Just run through, and they won't do anything. As long as we get in the train before they call security, we'll be fine," Sean said.

"What do you mean?" Thomas asked. I was glad he asked, because I wanted to ask the same question.

"We're going to take the subway. Just follow me," Sean said.

As Sean turned around, Thomas tapped his shoulder. I thought he was going to turn around and punch him, but he just looked at him calmly.

"Where are we going?" Thomas asked.

"To get that new game," he said.

I watched as Sean ran into the station and

jumped over the turnstile. I was waiting for someone to start yelling at him, but everything was silent. Following Thomas into the station, I noticed that the collector's booth was empty. I could tell that Thomas was just as nervous as I was.

"Just follow me, and copy me," I whispered to him. Sean was out of sight and earshot, so there was no way he would know what we were doing.

I walked over to the collector's booth, and pretended I was dropping change into the receptacle. I quickly walked through the turnstile. As I looked back, I saw Thomas doing the exact same thing.

Relief sweeping over me, I grabbed Thomas's shoulder before he could walk towards the platform.

"Why are you hanging out with Sean? He's a criminal. Did you steal those chips and that bottle of soda?" I asked him.

Shrugging my hand off of his shoulder, he ignored me. I watched as he made his way towards the platform, following the same path Sean had taken. I didn't know what to do, so I followed him. As we waited on the platform, I kept on looking around at everyone. Did they know that we didn't pay our fare? Would they report us? Would we be arrested? I tried to keep my emotions in checks. The last thing I wanted was to give Sean a reason to hurt me. As long as I stayed under the radar, I should be okay.

As the train pulled in to the station, I took in a deep breathe. Following Sean and Thomas into the train, I sat down and folded my hands in my lap. I only had to endure this until ten, and then I could go home. If I wasn't home by then, surely my mom would come looking for me. Right?

Keele

Observing my reflection in the mirror, I could tell that there was something missing. My hair was gelled and combed to the contours of my skull. My white shirt was freshly ironed and was buttoned right up to the bottom of my chin. My white slacks clung tightly to my thighs, but still allowed ample room to breathe. Everything was perfect; what was missing?

Turning my head from side to side, I studied my chin. My beard was shaved down to the edges of my chin, and both sides were uniform. My eyebrows had been meticulously trimmed the day before, so it couldn't be that. I stood looking at my reflection, trying to figure out what was missing.

"Trevor, your lunch is ready!" Mrs. Gusset called from downstairs.

I didn't answer her. I never did, and she never said anything to me about it. It wasn't that I didn't like her; I thought she was alright. I just didn't like responding to others.

Still staring at my reflection, I cocked my head to the left. I still could not figure out what was wrong with my reflection. Until I did, I could not leave. The seconds were ticking by on the clock, and I wasn't getting any closer to leaving the room.

"Oh dear," I said aloud to myself, "it seems likes we'll need to restart."

Stepping away from the mirror, I walked over to my bed. I carefully removed my white shirt, placed it on a hanger, buttoned it up, and hung it in my closet. I then took off my white slacks, placed then on a hanger, and hung them in my closet. I removed my white shoes by slipping them off, and carefully placed them near the room's door.

"Alright, dear," I said aloud, "let us get ready for the day."

I removed my white slacks from the closet and put them on. I unbuttoned my white shirt to free it from the hanger, and put it on myself. After I finished buttoning up the last button, all the way up to my chin, I walked over to my dresser. Carefully opening the second drawer, I removed a white pair of socks.

"Of course!" I exclaimed. "I forgot my white socks!"

Sitting on the edge of the bed, I put on my white socks. After pulling them as high up as they would go on my legs, I walked over to the door and picked up my shoes. Making my way back to the bed,

I sat down and slipped my feet effortlessly into the shoes.

I was pretty sure that I was perfectly dressed, but I would need to check my reflection in the mirror to make sure. Standing in front of the mirror, I observed my reflection. It was perfect.

Walking out of my room, I carefully closed my door. We weren't allowed to lock our bedroom doors here, but no one ever went into anyone else's room. No one that is, except for Robert and Edna. They would go into our rooms once a week to make sure it was clean and we had everything we needed. My room was always spotless; they never had to do any additional cleaning.

"Hi Trevor," Mica said to me, as he left his room.

I looked straight ahead and didn't respond. I hadn't seen Mica before he spoke to me. I wish I had. I wanted to greet him and tell him about the book I was reading, but I couldn't now. Maybe I could talk to him tomorrow.

I went down the stairs and straight into the kitchen. When Mrs. Gusset noticed me, she gave me a smile and told me to help myself to lunch. I grabbed a plate from the cupboard, and studied what she had cooked for today. There were chicken sandwiches, soup, and chicken wings. I couldn't tell what type of soup it was, so I just took a sandwich and seven chicken wings.

Seated at the kitchen table, I started eating my sandwich. It was good; it tasted like all the other chicken sandwiches Mrs. Gusset has made. When I finished with my sandwich, I started eating my chicken wings. They were full of sauce, but they weren't really spicy. I enjoyed spicy foods, but they didn't cook them here.

When I finished eating, I put the bones from my chicken wings into the compost bin, and brought my dishes to the sink. I really hated doing dishes; I didn't like the feel of the soap on my hands. Nevertheless, I had to do them if I wanted to stay here. All rules had to be followed, or else you wouldn't be allowed to stay here. Picking up my plate and the sponge from the sink, I started washing my plate. I wanted to stay here. I liked it here; I had a lot more freedom than the other two places I had been staying in over the last three years.

As soon as I finished washing the dishes, I wiped my hands on a hand towel until they were bone dry. I wanted to thank Mrs. Gusset for the meal, but I couldn't. Maybe tomorrow I would be able to. I walked past her, and started walking towards the living room.

As I entered the living room, I saw Pern sitting on the couch reading a book. He looked up when he saw me, but then immediately went back to his book. I liked Pern.

"Hi Pern, what are you reading?" I asked him.

I watched as he carefully placed a bookmark in his book, closed it, and placed it on his lap. He stared at me, but did not say anything

"It's okay, Pern. You can talk now," I said. He always waited to make sure I was done greeting him, before he started talking. I didn't mind it if someone spoke to me first, but I could not tolerate it if someone interrupted me.

"Hi Trevor. I don't know," he replied, as he picked up the book and looked at the cover. "I just found it here, so I decided to start reading it."

I silently counted to ten to make sure he was done talking. "What are you doing today?"

He waited a few seconds before responding. "I have to go to a job interview today. Margaret is coming to pick me up. She said to wear something professional, so I wore this," he said, as he looked down and pointed at his clothing.

I studied what he was wearing. He had on a pair of black pants that fell on top of a pair of black shoes. He wore a white shirt, and had a blue ties dangling in the middle.

"I like your white shirt," I told him.

He didn't say anything else. After a few minutes of silence, he picked up his book and started reading again. He forgot to ask me what I was doing today; he wasn't been reciprocal.

"Pern, do you want to know what I'm doing today," I asked him.

I watched as he carefully placed his bookmark back in his book, and placed it on his lap. "Yes, Trevor. What are you doing today?"

I silently counted to ten. "I'm going to work today. It's my first day. Margaret got me a job at a restaurant. I don't know what I'll be doing, but she said I'll get to make food for people," I told him.

After a slight pause—longer than the few seconds he usually took—he cocked his head to the side. "Aren't you worried that your clothes will get dirty?"

I silently counted to ten. "Why on earth would my clothes get dirty?" I asked him.

"Because they're white," he replied.

I shrugged my shoulders, and turned away from him. I was looking at the TV, even though it was closed. From the reflection it projected, I could see him picking his book back up and opening it to where the bookmark laid.

There was nothing wrong with my clothes. They wouldn't get dirty. I would be very careful. I looked down at my clothes to make sure they were still clean; they were.

I remained seated in the living room. I didn't really want to stay here—I would rather be in my room—but Margaret would be here soon. She didn't like having to wait for us to be ready. After a few more minutes, I heard the front door unlock and open.

"Hi Margaret!" I yelled out, before I even saw her. Sometimes she forgot the rules, and I wanted to make sure I'd be able to talk to her if I needed help with my new job.

"Hi Trevor. Hi Pern," she said, as she appeared in the living room. "Come on, we need to get going."

I got up and followed Margaret. I could hear Pern following behind me. We followed her out the door, and down the porch steps. We had been walking for at least five minutes before she started talking to us.

"Okay, listen up," she said. "This is today's schedule: we will be going to Trevor's new job, where you'll start training. Pern, I've lined up an interview for you with the same manager that hired Trevor. If everything goes well, you should start working tomorrow. All clear?"

"Yes, it's clear," I responded. I was so happy that I was able to respond to her today. Most of our helpers understood, but she sometimes got angry if I didn't respond to her.

"It's clear," Pern said, from behind me.

We continued walking until we arrived at the subway station. I really enjoyed taking the subway. We weren't allowed to take it alone, but as long as someone accompanied us, we could use it at least once a week.

Margaret handed us each a token, and led us to the collector's booth. I remembered how to do it, but I think Pern forgot. He looked really nervous and was trying to get me to go before him. I liked Pern, so I went ahead of him. Making sure he could see me, I dropped my token inside the box, and walked through the turnstile. A few seconds later, he followed me, and Margaret followed him.

When we arrived at the platform, I stood against the wall. I wasn't afraid of the train, but we always had to stand against the wall whenever we were on the platforms. Pern was standing beside me, and Margaret was standing in front of us.

As the train came into the station, there was a big burst of wind that came through. The wind felt so good. I always wanted to go closer, to feel the wind. But, that was not allowed. I would never break any rules; I would do everything they told me to do.

When the train stopped, Margaret motioned for us to follow her. We followed her into the train, and sat down where she told us to. As the doors closed, I closed my eyes in unison. I loved the feeling that ran through my body as the train sped through the tunnel.

Dundas West

The minutes on the clock were dragging by slowly. The last three times I had glanced at the clock, the numbers hadn't changed. I was waiting desperately until the day would be over. I did not want to be at work right now. Who would want to be stuck in an office when it was such a beautiful day outside?

"Caroline, do you want to come out with us for drinks?" Kathy asked from over my shoulder.

Swivelling around in my chair to face her, I set my face to what I hoped was a look of disappointment. "I'm so sorry. I wish you would have told me earlier. I just finished booking an appointment for right after work," I replied.

She shrugged her shoulders, seemingly unaffected. "Okay. Maybe next time. Have fun at your appointment," she said, as she walked away.

As soon as she disappeared from my field of vision, I let out a sigh of relief. At least once a week the Carbons would ask me if I wanted to go out with them. The first time they invited me, I gleefully accepted the invitation. I had just started working here a month prior, and I was eager to make friends.

That was my first mistake.

The Carbons consisted of Kathy, Michelle, Ariana, Lea, and Jennifer. Although they were all physically unique—Ariana was easily heavier than Kathy and Lea combined—they all acted the same. If two of them come into the room holding a different opinion, one of them quickly changes their mind to reflect that of the group. They're nothing but carbon copies of each other; none of them really seemed to have anything upstairs.

When I had gone out with them, we ended up going to a karaoke bar. I wasn't ever really fond of karaoke, but I thought I would give it another try. I spent the whole night nursing two beers, while they kept on pounding shot after shot, drink after drink.

When the bill came, I pulled out a twenty to pay for my share, which was more than enough. Although I wasn't in a position to see my face, I can just imagine the priceless look I must have given them when they announced that my share of the bill came to $68.25. At first I thought it was just a mistake, and pointed out that I had only ordered two beers. Lea flat-out told me they split the bill evenly, regardless of what everyone ordered individually.

I swivelled from side to side in my chair,

remembering that night. I had hated them from that day, but never made any displays of outward aggression. Regardless of how I felt about them, they were still my coworkers. And at five to one, they sure could make my life a living hell if they wanted to.

I silently chuckled to myself, and shook my head. There was no point in holding grudges. Grudges didn't do anything. They didn't get your money back. They didn't make you feel better. However, revenge might.

Continuing to swivel from side to side in my chair, a thought started forming in my head. What if I attempted to get revenge on them? How would I be able to go about it? Obviously, I wouldn't be able to do anything at work. It would have to be after work, off of company property.

Getting out of my chair, I made my way over to Kathy's desk. She was chatting away with Jennifer, not even pretending to be working.

I mustered up the cheeriest voice I could. "Hey Kathy!" I exclaimed. "You know what, I'll take you up on that offer. I still have to go to my appointment, but I can meet you guys afterwards."

Both Kathy and Jennifer started squealing at the same time. They quickly hugged each other, and then got out of their chairs to hug me.

"This is going to be amazing," Kathy squealed.

"We're going to have so much fun," Jennifer chimed in.

"Oh my god! I can't wait to tell the others. They will be so excited," Kathy said.

I tried to muster as must gleefulness as I could, hugging them back with the same force they were using. It seemed liked they were buying it.

"So," I said, "if you just tell me where we're going, I can meet you guys when I'm done at my appointment."

"Do you know where we're going today?" Kathy asked Jennifer.

Jennifer squinted her eyes as if she was deep in thought, and then replied to Kathy. "No, I don't know. I'll go ask Ariana."

I watched as Jennifer quickly made her way across the aisle, disappearing behind a row of cubicles. I turned my attention back to Kathy, and realized just how uncomfortable it was being with just her. I could tolerate all of them together. But alone? That was definitely not my favourite position to be in.

Kathy was staring at me with such intensity. It

made me feel really uncomfortable. I tried to flash a few reassuring smiles on my face, but I don't think it was working.

"You look a bit pale, Caroline. Are you sure you're okay?" she asked me. She was now staring intensely into my face, her nose barely an inch away from mine.

I faked a sneeze and turned my head away from her. The sudden movement had caused her to step backwards, freeing up my personal space.

"Sorry about that," I said. "I'm okay. I guess it was just a sneeze waiting to escape."

"Oh, okay," she replied, with a look of confusion on her face. "So anyways, what's your appointment for?"

What was the nature of my appointment? I hadn't thought that far. I tried thinking of something, but came up blank. She kept on staring intently at me, so I faked another sneeze.

"Oh my god, are you allergic to something?" she asked, stepping even further away from me. That wasn't my main goal, but I would take it.

"Sorry again. I don't know what it is. Maybe there's dust," I said. "Anyways, my appointment is with..." I struggled to find an answer. "It's with...it's with my husband."

"Oh," Kathy said, "I never knew you were married."

I wasn't. "Oh, I'm not. I mean, I won't be soon. We have an appointment for our divorce."

None of this really sounded convincing in my head, but she seemed to have bought it. She was nodding her head in an apologetic way, and leaned in close to give me a hug. I guess that was a waste, freeing up my personal space.

As she continued squishing me, I spotted Jennifer heading towards us. Finally, maybe a little sanity would be restored.

"Here you go," Jennifer said, as she handed me a piece of paper. "Ariana wrote down directions for you. We're going right after work, but we'll be staying for most of the night."

"And don't worry," Kathy chimed in. "We won't leave before you get there."

"Awesome," I said, mustering up the little cheer that was left within me.

Glancing at the clock, I noticed that the work day had ended three minutes ago. Excusing myself, I walked over to my desk, closed my computer, and made my way out of the building.

I started walking in the usual direction I use to get home, until I was out of sight from the building. After making sure that none of the Carbons had followed me, I continued walking down the street. I was looking for a specific store, and hoped that I wouldn't have to venture too far.

After walking a couple of blocks, I finally found a store that might sell what I needed. As I opened to the door to the pharmacy, the little bells tied to the top of the door chimed. A man in a white coat behind the counter looked up, and gave me a smile.

I wasn't even going to bother looking around the store. The easiest way to get what I needed was to ask. Approaching him, I tried to display a look of friendliness and concern.

"Hi, I'm hoping you can help me. You see, my roommate has really bad constipation. And I mean, really really bad. He refuses to see a doctor, so I'm trying to be a good friend to help him out. What would you recommend to, you know, just give him that little extra boost to make everything..." I let my sentence trail.

"I have just the thing for you," he said, as he made his way around the counter.

I followed him to an aisle, and watched as he displayed three different laxative products to me. They all pretty much looked the same to me.

"Which one is stronger?" I asked him.

He replaced two of the boxes back on the shelf, and handed me the remaining one from his hand. "This one is the strongest. Make sure he's home and near a bathroom before taking it. If you only have one bathroom in your place, you might want to do your business before giving it to him."

"I better grab two," I said, grabbing another package from the shelf. "You know, just in case."

After thanking him and paying for the laxatives, I made my way out the store. The first phase of my plan was already complete. For phase two, I needed to get to the Carbons. Slipping the piece of paper Jennifer had handed me with the directions, I tried to figure out how far the bar was.

After a few quiet minutes of internal deliberation, I took out my phone and punched in the address into my GPS locator map. The bar was a 42 minute walk; it would be much quicker to take public transit. Pocketing my phone, I made my way to the nearest subway station.

Arriving at the subway station, I paid my fare

and made my way to the platform. As I waited for the train, I glanced into my bag. Two packs of laxatives would be more than enough. Heck, even one pack would be enough. But if you're out for revenge, why not do it with a bang?

When the train pulled into the station, I took a window seat and laid my head against the window. An eye for an eye? If someone takes my eye, I'm coming after their eyes, nose, mouth, and everything within my reach. I could not wait to exact my revenge.

Lansdowne

When I woke up, I was already three hours late. I used to care about being late, but I don't anymore. After being promoted to the position of manager last year, I was able to get away with anything and everything I wanted. My supervisor only came to visit once a month, and I always received a heads up at least three days in advance. None of my employees would dare say a word; where else would they have to turn to, in this economy?

Getting out of bed, I lazily walked over to the bathroom. My hair was a mess. I ruffled it with my hands a bit, but it just got messier. Turning on the tap in the tub, I allowed the water to run through the showerhead for a few seconds. Happy with the temperature, I stuck my head under the water, soaking every inch of my hair.

With my eyes closed, I felt for the handle and turned off the water. I shook my head from side to side, trying to remove most of the excess water. Reaching my hand out to the left of me, I blindly grabbed at various items until I found a towel. Drying my hair, I walked back over to the mirror.

I rinsed out my mouth with water, and flattened my wet hair against my head. I thought I looked pretty decent, as always, so I went back into my room and got dressed. I took out a pair of trousers and a button up shirt from my closet. I preferred sweatpants, but I had to shows them all who was boss. Grabbing a red tie from my dresser, I finished my ensemble.

I looked at my reflection in the mirror for a couple of minutes, before being satisfied that I looked great. Grabbing my car keys and my phone, I made my way to work.

Once I arrived at work, I walked into my office and closed the door. I didn't want anyone bothering me until I had settled in. The red light on my phone was flashing, indicating that I had a message. I didn't really feel like working right now, but I might as well get it out of the way. I pressed PLAY on the answering machine, and sat back in my chair. It was most likely a nonsense call.

"Hi Matt. This is Clara. I've been trying to reach you for the last three weeks. I still haven't been paid, and I'm wondering—" Before the message was through, I deleted it from the answering machine.

Leaning back in my chair, I laughed and

shook my head. What a dumb broad. She was crazy if she thought I was going to be paying her. The bitch had the audacity to quit and file a complaint against me. She wasn't going to be seeing a penny any time soon.

That was the only message on the answering machine, so I got up and opened my door. I might as well give the vultures easy access. They needed direction, or else they'd just stumble and fall all over each other.

"Kimberly," I beckoned through the door frame.

I watched as she got up from her desk and made her way towards me. I knew she despised me; I read a few emails she sent to Brent about me. That was alright. It was always more satisfactory when you knew they hated you, but did what you said anyways.

"Yes?" she said, as she approached me.

"Get me a sandwich from the cafeteria, and an orange juice," I dictated to her.

She stood motionless in front of me. Why were they all so dumb? They couldn't even follow simple commands.

"Now," I said to her. "Go get it now."

I could see her fidgeting. "Sure, I just need the

money to get it."

I laughed. "I'll pay you back later."

"But, you still owe me—"

I cut her off. "Go get it. Now."

I watched as she scrambled to the door, and disappeared as it closed behind her. I couldn't wait to get my hands on that sandwich. I was starving.

Making my way back to my office, I sat down in my chair. Turning on my computer, I browsed to my favourite social media site. I could very well kill the rest of the day on here.

I heard a knock at my door and looked up. I was expecting to see Kimberly with my food, but it was Shaun.

"Yes?" I asked.

"There's someone here to see you," she said.

"Well," I said, with a deliberate hint of venom in my voice, "who is it?" I was growing impatient with these morons I had to work with.

"I don't know. They didn't say," she replied.

I looked at her for a few moments, and then directed my energy back at my computer screen. If she didn't know who it was, I didn't know if I could see them. Shaun was still standing in the doorway. She cleared her throat, a pathetic attempt to get my attention.

I slowly focused my attention on her. "Yes?"

She was shifting her weight from leg to leg. "What should I tell them?"

I sighed loudly, and waved her out of my office. She didn't waste a moment, and was gone within a matter of seconds. I turned my attention back to my computer. I was on my ex-girlfriend's social media profile. I was browsing through her pictures, and noticed a few of them with Hector, her supposed new boyfriend. He was such a douche. She was probably a lesbian anyway.

I started feeling stressed out. Getting out of my chair, I walked out of my office and made my way outside. Leaning my back against the wall of the building, I took a cigarette out of my pocket and lit it. The first drag was calming, the nicotine hitting my system.

As I took in the view, my stomach started grumbling. Finishing the rest of my cigarette, I threw the butt on the ground. I squished it under my shoe, and started walking back towards the building's entrance. If Kimberly knew what was good for her, she'd have my sandwich on my desk by the time I got back to my office.

As I made my way towards the front door, I noticed a car idling in the parking lot. I walked over to the car, pulling up my sleeves as I grew nearer. Wrapping my knuckle against the window, I waited until the driver wound it down.

"Excuse me, what are you doing here? This is private property. You can't just come here and use our parking lot," I said to the man sitting in the driver's seat.

I looked at him, waiting for a response. After a few moments of silence, I noticed that the passenger behind him had rolled down his window.

"Is that him?" he asked the driver.

"Yep," replied the driver.

I was started to get angry. "Am I who? Who do you think I am? Who the hell are you?" I balled my fists at my sides.

Before I had a chance to swing a punch at the driver, I felt someone grab me. Caught off guard, I felt myself being pulled through the passenger side window. My body scrapped against the frame, causing pain to shoot throughout. I tried to escape, but was overpowered.

As the rest of my body was pulled into the car, I felt the car shake. We were now moving. I was being kidnapped by a bunch of thugs, for god knows what.

"What the hell are you doing?" I shouted. "Get off of me, let me go!" I screamed at the man beside me.

No one responded to me. I wanted to continue shouting and screaming, but slowly realized that it might be best to just keep my mouth closed for now. I didn't know who they were, or what they wanted. If they wanted to rob me, I'd just give them my money and take back whatever they took from the petty cash box at work.

The car suddenly stopped, and the driver got out. He opened the rear passenger door, and grabbed me by my shirt collar. Yanking me out of the car, he threw me against the ground. I looked around, and figured out we were in an alley of some sort. I couldn't tell where we were.

"Do you know who I am?" the driver asked me.

Looking up at him from the ground, I shook my head from side to side. That obviously wasn't the answer he was looking for, since he kicked me in the stomach. Doubling over, I clutched my midsection in pain.

"Let me jog your memory," he said. "Do you

remember Clara? You know, the woman who worked for you for two months under abusive circumstances. When she left, you didn't pay her. She's been calling you for her paycheque, over and over and over again. You just ignore her calls. Why is that?"

I couldn't believe Clara put them up to this. That bitch would pay. I closed my eyes and clutched at my stomach again, bracing myself for another impact. When none came, I slowly opened my eyes. I opened them just in time to see a boot coming towards my face.

"Felix, take over," I heard the driver say.

Within a matter of seconds, I felt the repeated pounding of kicks lobbed at every area of my body. I was burning with pain. The onslaught continued, while the driver grabbed my head in between his hands placing us face to face. Crouched over me, he spat in my face.

"You see, sweet Clara doesn't know that we're here. She's busy sitting at home, trying to get a hold of you. I tried to think of a reason why you would steal money from someone who worked for you. The only thing I could come up with is respect. You see, you lack respect for others. Out of the good fortune of our hearts, we're here to help you learn," he said.

He dropped my head back down to the ground, as Felix continued to kick me. I don't know how long they continued beating me for, but it felt like an eternity. I felt as if I was about to succumb to the temptation of unconsciousness, when they suddenly stopped. I didn't risk any movement, not wanting to provoke them. Everything hurt anyways, so it was better to just lie still. After a few minutes of silence, I heard the driver start talking.

"You listen now, and you listen good," the driver said. "You're going to call Clara and apologize for being such scum. You are going to pay her what she's owed, but double. We'll call it interest. If I hear that she hasn't received her money by the end of the week, we might have to come back and pay you a another little visit. Understand?"

I tried nodding my head, but pain shot up my spine. I felt another kick aimed at my legs, and yelled out in pain.

"Yes!" I shouted. "Yes, I understand."

I heard the sound of car doors closing, and an engine starting up. It sounded like the car had left, but I stayed motionless for about five minutes, just to make sure. When I thought it was clear, I slowly made my way up, off the ground. Everything hurt, as

I put myself in a standing position.

I didn't even know where I was. I started walking in the street, looking for anything that was familiar. Every step that I took hurt, but I couldn't stop walking. I didn't recognize where I was, but I recognized a subway station a block away. I continued walking, breathing heavily as each step I took shot pain throughout my body.

Arriving at the station, a few people started staring at me. Although they were staring, none of them offered help. Screw them; I didn't need anyone's help anyways. I reached into my pocket for my wallet. Luckily, they didn't take it. I paid my fare, and made my way towards the platform.

As I waited for the train to arrive, I leaned my weight against the wall. It alleviated some of the pain, but didn't really make that much of a difference overall. My whole body was aching.

When the train pulled into the station, I walked inside as fast as my body would allow and sat down, taking up two seats. Amidst all the pain, I felt my stomach rumbling. My sandwich better be on my desk by the time I get back to work.

Dufferin

Looking at my reflection in the mirror, I watched as a bead of sweat made its way from the top of my brow to the side of my nose. A few more jarring movements and it slid to the top of my lip. I could taste the saltiness of my sweat, as it rolled across by lips to the bottom of my chin. Only ten more to go, and I would beat my record.

I raised the entire weight of my body with my two hands. My muscles were growing tired. Burning and aching, I pushed through the pain. Only nine more to go. A bellow was released from deep within my diaphragm. Only eight more to go.

I was struggling to bring myself back up to the starting position. My arms shook violently, as I tried to force myself back to the initial push up position. I could feel my body slowly rising, as every muscle fibre in my arms struggled to support my weight. Just as I reached the peak of the push up, I suddenly collapsed onto the floor.

I remained lying head first on the floor, feeling a pool of sweat collecting around my body. I hadn't beat my record, but I had done pretty well for today. I waited a few more minutes, until I felt the energy return to my body. Slowly rising from the floor, I stood in front of the mirror.

Observing my physique, a smile beamed on my face. Don't get me wrong; I'm not arrogant, narcissistic, or egotistical. I was merely admiring the results of consistent strength training. I had already surpassed all the minimum requirements, but that wasn't enough. I wanted to shatter all records, to become the best I could be.

I had planned on going out for a jog immediately after, but my body was still reeling from the grueling workout I just submitted it to. Deciding to postpone my jog, I made my way to the bathroom. I peeled my sweat-drenched clothing off my body, and laid it on the towel rack. Turning on the water, I jumped into the shower.

After I dried myself off and got dressed in clean clothes, I felt a lot better. I was still feeling a bit too tired to go out for a jog, so spread myself on my bed, allowing the soft pillow to gently caress the sides of my face. Reaching out my hand and grabbing my computer from my desk, I automatically browsed to the Canadian Armed Forces website.

I spent a few minutes scrolling through the

site. I had visited the site every single day for the past couple of years. I knew almost everything they had on there by heart. After seeing that nothing new had been added, I clicked over to my email to check if I had received any new messages. After deleting two spam messages, I closed my computer and placed it to my side.

Closing my eyes, I tried to imagine myself in Basic Training. I imagined blowing all of my training officers away, leaving them in awe of my talent. I imagined breaking every single record, of never showing any sign of weakness. I would be the strongest recruit they had. I would be the best recruit they had.

A few years ago, I had no idea what I wanted to do with my life. Everyone around me was trying to push me in a specific direction, which just led me to retreat within myself. At that time, I didn't know who I was. Actually, let me rephrase that. I did know who I was; I just didn't like who I was.

Growing up, I had always been the fat kid in class. From elementary school to secondary school, I was bullied on an almost daily basis. It didn't help that I was also shy, so I never spoke back to any of my tormentors. Regardless of how they treated me, I never cried. They could call me any names they wanted, they could beat me until I bled, but they could never make me cry.

As I was trying to figure out what I wanted to do with my life, I stumbled onto an army forum online. From that day, I had been enthralled with anything and everything that had to do with the military. It was an honourable thing to be able to call yourself a soldier, and I wanted nothing more than to hold that honour.

As you could guess, I encountered a rather large problem with my newfound goal. There was no way I would pass the physical requirements. At that time, I could barely do two push ups without crashing to the ground. And forget running. Even running a few seconds to catch the bus knocked the wind out of me.

I knew that I wouldn't be able to get recruited the way I was. So, I made a plan. And from that day forward, I spent every single day working on my plan. I slowly incorporated strength training into my day, until it went from fifteen minutes to two hours at a time. I started walking, until I was able to progress to running. I hadn't rushed into anything. I took everything slowly, making sure that my body was adapting correctly.

Today, I was in the best shape of my life. Heck, I was in the best shape of any person I had ever met in person. I continued training every day, and created myself into the beast I had become. My muscles were bulging. My biceps were bigger now, than they were when I was fat. Instead of being mushy and fluid with movement, they were hard and solid.

Closing my eyes, I took a deep breath. The moment would soon be upon me: the moment where I found out if all my hard work had paid off. Next Monday, I had an appointment with a recruiter. I knew that I would most likely have to apply online, but I wanted to make sure I did everything correctly.

Even though I had long ago achieved all physical requirements, I was still nervous. What if they didn't like me? What if I wasn't smart enough? Even though I hadn't gone to college or university, I was still plenty smart. I didn't want to go to school—secondary school had been more than enough for me—but I would go if they told me to. I would do anything they told me to.

Feeling a bit more relaxed, I felt ready to go out for my jog. I grabbed my hydration belt from my dresser, and tied it around my waist. Grabbing my water bottles out of the fridge, I placed them snuggly within the confines of my belt. I slipped my wallet into my back pocket, and grabbed my phone. Locking the door behind me, I headed into the open street.

My routine usually consisted of walking one block, before I started running. Today, I didn't have the patience to wait. Propelling myself with my feet, I accelerated until I achieved a consistent running pace. The thought of running used to disgust me; now it filled me up with joy.

As I ran down the street, I looked around. If you focused your eyesight straight ahead, you always saw the same things. The same buildings. The same cars. The same people. But if you focused your attention just a bit higher, there were infinite possibilities when looking at the sky. I could easily lose a few hours just looking at up at clouds during the day, or at stars during the night. It had taken me a while, but I have mastered focusing my attention between paying attention to where I was running, to the obstacles in front of me, to the magnificent beauty of the sky.

As I ran past another block, I started feeling thirsty. Grabbing a bottle from my hydration belt, I allowed the cold liquid to guzzle down my throat. Replacing the empty bottle in its spot, I wiped my mouth with the back of my hand.

My feet continued pounding the pavement. I watched the clouds slowly drift into a new formation. The movement was hypnotic and relaxing. I continued to occasionally glance ahead of me to make sure I didn't run into any obstacles or go through a 'no walking' signal, but the majority of my attention was focused on the clouds up above.

I continued running, until I had covered approximately ten kilometers. That would be enough for today. Slowing down my pace, I looked around and took in my surroundings. There was a small independent grocery store a few steps ahead. Making my way to the store, I wiped the sweat from my face.

Inside the grocery store, I walked around the store before deciding on what I wanted. I grabbed a carton of strawberries, a bottle of peach smoothie, a box of granola bars, and a chocolate bar. After I paid for my purchase, I walked for a few more minutes, trying to orient myself. It only took a few minutes to locate a subway station.

Walking into the subway station, I paid my fare and made my way to the platform. Holding my purchased groceries, I mentally mapped out the route I would need to take to head to the beach. It was a beautiful day outside; it would be great to enjoy it to its fullest.

As I waited for the train to arrive, I daydreamed about lying on the beach and looking up at the clouds. I didn't have a towel or blanket, but that would be okay. The sand would probably stick to my sweat, but that could easily be remedied by a quick dip in the water.

When the train pulled into the station, I walked in and stood in front of the doors opposite from the side I had entered. I never sat on the subway, streetcar, or bus. Standing on a moving vehicle allowed me to work on my balance. There was nothing I wouldn't do or try to craft myself into the best of the best.

Ossington

I was sitting in the back of the class, copying down word for word the slides that the professor was projecting onto the projection screen. I couldn't really focus on what he was saying, but as long as I wrote everything down I would be okay. I noticed that Callie highlighted one of the sentences she was copying down. I must have missed something. Grabbing a highlighter from my bag, I highlighted the same passage she had.

By the time the professor clicked over to the last slide, my hands were cramped up from writing. I really hated taking notes, but I had no choice. I wasn't doing very well in this class, and my parents were threatening to cancel my summer vacation. As long as I passed this class, I would be okay.

Since there wasn't anything else left to copy down, I tossed my notebook and pens into my bag. I waited until a few people started to get up and leave, and followed them. As I exited the classroom, a wave of relief swept over me. I wouldn't have to step foot in there until next week.

As people were milling about, I tried to look

for someone I knew. I had purposefully sat away from my friends so that I could concentrate, although I don't think that had really helped. The only person I recognized was Callie, but I didn't really know her that well. I didn't feel like sticking around in the hallway, so I headed over to the student center.

"Todd!" I heard someone shouting my name, and turned around to see who it was. As I got closer, I made out the distinct shape of Mercer.

Mercer was one of my best friends. We had gone to secondary school together, and now to the same university. Since we both had different majors, we never really had class together. That didn't stop us from goofing around on campus.

"Hey man. I thought you didn't have classes today?" I asked him, as I moved his backpack from the chair it was occupying and sat down.

"No, no class. Just finished working on a group project. Wanna see what we've got so far?" he asked me.

"Honestly," I replied, "no. Put that away. I have three hours to burn before my next class. What do you want to do?"

Mercer chuckled as he grabbed his backpack and put his things away. "All right, buddy. What do you want to do?"

"I just asked you that," I said, as I lightly punched him in his arm. "Come on, then. Let's just hop in your car and go for a drive."

I followed Mercer out into the parking lot and into his car. His car was okay. It wasn't as good as mine, but it drove well. I had a beautiful souped-up car that my parents had taken away from me. Even if they hadn't taken it away, I still couldn't drive it until my licence was no longer suspended.

As we cruised down the highway, I opened my window. The fast wind felt amazing against my face. I looked around at the other cars on the road, losing myself in the self-induced hypnotic rhythm.

When I snapped out of my daze, I realized we had exited the highway and were now driving in the city. I didn't really recognize where we were, but that didn't matter. After a few more minutes of driving, Mercer pulled into the driveway of a small house. He parked the car, and got out. I followed him.

"Where are we?" I asked him.

"Ashley's. I told her I'd swing by later today. You didn't decide where you wanted to go, so here we are," he said.

I let out a sigh. "Great, so now I'm the third

wheel?"

"Just relax," he said.

We walked up to the door, and he knocked lightly. After a few seconds, the door swung open and revealed Ashley. She was okay looking. Not my type, but Mercer liked her. They weren't exactly dating, but he was doing everything he could to push them in that direction.

"Oh, he's here?" Ashley said, as she noticed me standing on her porch.

"Hi to you too," I said, as I pushed my way past her and into the house. I could hear them following behind, closing and locking the door.

The television was turned on to a World War II documentary. I quickly located the remote on the couch, and changed the station.

"Hey, I was watching that!" Ashley screamed, as I plopped myself down on the couch.

"Why don't you go spend some time with your boyfriend?" I shot back at her.

Even though I couldn't see Mercer, I knew that his face must have been beet red. I momentarily felt bad about what I said, but that quickly passed. He was a big boy; he would get over it.

I heard her stomp her feet and let out a small

suppressed yell. "You know Todd, you're such a jerk. Come on, Mercer. Let's go upstairs."

I listened as their footsteps got further and further away, until they disappeared into quietness. The only sound I heard was the television, just the way it should be. I scrolled through the stations until I found something to watch.

Feeling thirsty, I got up and went into the kitchen. I grabbed a six-pack that from the fridge, and a bag of chips from the counter. The beer wasn't really that high quality, but it would do. Plopping myself back onto the couch, I opened a beer and chugged half of it down in one go.

By the time the cartoon I was watching had finished, I was down to the last two beers in the pack. Letting out a large burp, I fished my hand into the bag of chips. Pulling up only crumbs, I crumpled the bag and tossed it onto the coffee table. I was still hungry, so I went into the kitchen to find something else to eat.

As I entered the kitchen once more, I quickly looked around for easy access food. There wasn't anything tempting, except for a bowl of bananas and apples on the counter. That didn't seem appetizing; I would pass that. I opened the fridge, and rummaged through a few containers. I found a container with some left over lasagna, and grabbed that.

Placing the container in the microwave, I nuked it for a few minutes. When the microwave beeped, I grabbed the container. I didn't anticipate how hot it would be, and the container dropped from my grip. As the lasagna splattered all over the floor and my pants, I swore out loud.

"Oh, just great!" I shouted, starring at the orange stain forming on my pants.

I walked into the living room and took off my pants. Holding the stain closer to my face, I tried to see if I would be able to remove it. I don't know quite what I was expecting to deduce from holding it that close to my face, but I couldn't figure out if I could take it out or not. Turning my attention towards the staircase, I quickly made my way upstairs, taking the stairs two at a time.

The first room I came upon was empty. I ruffled through the closet and drawers, but all of the clothing was female. I left that room and continued walking down the hallway. When I got to the next room, I could hear some light talking and laughing. It looked like Mercer was putting his moves on Ashley. Throwing the door open, I walked into the room.

"Tood, what the hell?" Mercer said.

"Why are you in your boxers?" Ashley asked.

They were both lying down on the bed, but had immediately jumped up as soon as I entered the room. I looked down at my boxers, and chuckled to myself.

"Won't you look at that, it looks like I am in my boxers. See, there's a funny story there. I made some lasagna, and it fell on my pants. Do you have another pair of pants I can wear?" I asked, giving Ashely a coy smile.

"Are you kidding me? That was my lunch! Get out! Just get out!" she yelled at me, throwing a pillow in my face.

Ducking the rest of the items she started throwing at me, I motioned for Mercer to come with me. "Come on, let's go back to campus."

He shook his head. "No. Sorry, but I'm going to stay here with Ashley. You're being kind of a jerk, you know."

"Just 'kind of'? More like a full-blown jerk," Ashley said, as she threw a book at me.

"How am I supposed to get back to campus?" I asked Mercer.

"Figure it out," he said. "I'll see you on

campus tomorrow."

"Fine, whatever," I said, storming out of the door.

As I ran down the stairs, I felt anger towards Mercer and Ashley. Whatever; it didn't matter. I could find my own way to campus. I didn't want to ride in his stupid car anyways. I retrieved my pants and put them back on. I grabbed the remnants of the six-pack, and left Ashley's house.

I couldn't remember the way we had turned into the street, so it took me a while to find my way to a major street I actually recognized. Opening one of the beers—popping the cap off with my teeth—I walked down the street until I found a subway station. When I finally found a subway station, I stood outside and chugged down the rest of the bottle. I threw the bottle into the garbage, along with the six-pack's cardboard box. I stuck the last bottle of beer in my back pocket, and made my way into the station.

I paid my fare and went over to the platform. Leaning against the wall, I grabbed the bottle of beer from my pocket and opened it. I chugged it down, trying to finish it before the train came into the station. As the last drop hit my lips, I lobbed the bottle onto the track and watched as it shattered. A few seconds later, the headlights of the incoming train were shining through the tunnel's opening.

As I got onto the train, I stretched my legs onto the seat in front of me. Checking my watch, I realized I would be late for my class. It didn't really bother me. I was doing fine in that class. As long as I managed to squeak by, my summer vacation wouldn't be in danger.

Christie

I was waiting for Beth outside, in front of the school. The bell had rung a while ago, and I was one of the only students still out here. Jacob was waiting for his parents to pick him up, and Amber was waiting for her mom, who happened to be a teacher.

I glanced through the window of the school's front door, hoping to see any hint that Beth was on her way out. I didn't know what she was doing. What was it that was taking her so long to do? She told me she had to go get something important, and that she would be outside shortly.

I heard a car and saw Jacob's parents stop in front of the school. He said bye to Amber, but not to me. It didn't really bother me. We weren't really friends anyways. As I watched the car drive off and disappear into the distance, I heard the front door swing open. Turning around, I saw Beth running through the doors.

"What took you so long?" I asked her.

"I'll show you in a bit," she said, as she started walking away from the school.

We walked for a few minutes in complete

silence. I was eager to find out what it was she was keeping from me, but there would be no use trying to pry it out of her. When we arrived at the intersection, she started walking straight, instead of turning left as we usually did.

"Hey, where are you going?" I asked her, alarmed at our sudden change in direction. "The subway's that way."

She didn't answer me, but continued walking. I followed her, hoping that she wouldn't be going too far. My parents weren't really strict when it came to getting home, but I had to be reasonable. If I took too long to get home, they might start getting worried.

Following Beth, we entered a park that was empty. At first I thought she wanted to go on the swings—one of her favourite activities—but she continued walking past them, into the opening of a bunch of trees.

She walked into the trees, until we were hidden from view. I was starting to get scared, but I didn't let it show. I didn't want Beth thinking that I was a wuss.

"Do you like Zoe?" she asked me? Zoe was in our class, and we hung out with her all the time. Her parents didn't let her take the subway, so she had to take the school bus home.

"Yes," I replied. I was confused as to why she was asking me. At first I thought that her birthday was coming up, but I remembered that we had had a sleepover for her birthday two months ago.

"No, you don't," she replied.

"Why?" I asked her, taken aback. "I thought you liked her too?"

Ignoring me, Beth took off her backpack and rested it against her legs on the ground. Opening up her bag, she rummaged until she found what she was looking for, and pulled out a folded sheet of paper.

"Look at this," she said, as she unfolded the sheet of paper and handed it to me. "Does that look like someone who's a friend?"

I took the piece of paper she gave me and looked at it. It was an email message from Zoe to Sarah, who was also in our class. The email was mostly about a group project they were doing, but I immediately knew why Beth was mad. Near the end, Zoe had written "Beth is such a loser. No boy in school will ever want to date her."

Handing the paper back to her, I didn't say anything. I didn't know what to say.

"Well, aren't you going to say something," she

said, angrily.

"Sorry. I don't know. Maybe she just said that, but she didn't mean it," I said.

"Oh, look at you always sticking up for everyone. Are you my friend, or what?" she asked.

I vigorously shook my head up and down. "Yes, yes. Zoe's the loser."

She put the paper back in her bag, and started rummaging for something else. She started pulling something out of her bag, but I couldn't quite make out what it was. It was shiny and metallic, and seemed pretty heavy.

"Beth, is that the pencil sharpener from the classroom?" I asked her, immediately recognizing the object once it was fully emerged from her bag.

She nodded her head, and handed it to me. I grabbed it in my hands, unsure of what to do. She had stolen from school. We could get expelled for that. What if we got caught? I didn't want to be suspended.

"Why did you steal the pencil sharpener?" I asked her, as I tried handing it back to her.

"Don't worry about it. I didn't steal it. I'll bring it back tomorrow," she said.

"But, I don't understand," I said, trying to

comprehend what she was saying. "If you didn't want to steal it and you're just going to bring it back tomorrow, why did you take it?"

Instead of answering me, she placed her bag on the ground and sat down on top of it. She motioned for me to do the same, so I complied. Once I was sitting down, she grabbed the pencil sharpener from me and ran her hands over it.

"You're my friend, right? My best friend?" she asked me.

"Of course," I said.

"Zoe really hurt me. And you know how Sarah is. She'll tell everyone that I'm a loser, and no one will want to be my friend," she said, staring at her reflection in the glare of the sharpener.

"But I'm your friend. I'll always be your friend," I said, trying to reassure her.

"That's not the point," she said, turning towards me and shooting me a glare.

I hated it when she glared at me. I looked down and stared at my shoes. I didn't know what to say, so I just stayed quiet. I didn't want to say the wrong thing again.

"Can you do something for me?" she asked me. Her voice was much gentler than it was a moment ago.

"Sure," I replied, eager to please.

"Can you get back at Zoe for me? She really hurt me," she said.

I didn't say anything, because I didn't know how to answer. Beth would most likely want me to ignore Zoe and be mean to her. I liked Zoe, and I didn't want to do that. I didn't think I would be able to.

"Well?" she prodded, growing impatient. "Are you going to help me or not?"

"Yes," I said. The word slipped out of my mouth, completely bypassing my brain.

"Good. Zoe invited me to a sleepover tonight. Her mom's going to drive us both to school tomorrow morning. Call your mom and ask if you can come," she said. She took out her cellphone from her pocket, and handed it to me.

"You guys were going to have a sleepover without me?" I asked, hurt.

"That's not the point. Just call you mom and ask," she replied.

"But, I thought you didn't like Zoe anymore? Why do you want to go on a sleepover?" I didn't understand Beth sometimes. She didn't always make sense.

"Just call!" she screamed at me.

I opened her phone and dialled home. After a couple of rings, my mom picked up.

"Hi honey," she said. "Is everything okay?"

"Yes, mom. I'm with Beth. Can I go to Zoe's house for a sleepover tonight? Beth is going too. Her mom's going to bring us home," I said. I didn't even care if she said no. I wasn't even sure if I wanted to go.

"Okay, honey. Just make sure you call me once you get to Zoe's house," she said.

"Okay. Thanks, mom," I said, as I hung up the phone.

As I handed Beth her phone back, a feeling of dread washed over me. I didn't know what she was thinking, and I didn't know how she wanted me to get back at Zoe for her.

"She said yes," I said.

"Good," Beth replied. "When she's asleep, we'll wake up. Take this," she said, handing me the pencil sharpener. "Hit her in the face, and break her nose. She'll be sleeping, so she won't know who did it. Oh! Just push her off the bed after, and she'll think she fell down and broke her nose."

The excitement and glee with which she was telling me her plan scared me. Her eyes were wide open, and there was a smile on her face. She looked happy.

"You want me to hit her in the face?" I asked. Bringing up the pencil sharpener to her eye level, I added, "With this?"

"Yeah. What's the big problem? I thought you said you would do it?" she replied.

"But, why can't you do it? If she's going to be sleeping and she won't know who it is, why can't you do it?" I asked.

"That's not the point!" she shouted. "You said you would do it. You have to do it."

"What if you poke out her eye? Or give her brain damage? Or kill her?" I asked her, in disbelief. I couldn't believe what she was asking me to do.

"Are you going to do it, or not?" she asked me.

I jumped up from the ground, and grabbed my backpack. Slinging it over my pack, I quickly walked away from her. As the distance between us grew larger, I remembered the pencil sharpener I was holding in my hands. I tossed it in her general direction, so it would hit the ground beside her.

"I'll see you at school tomorrow," I said to her,

trying to close the distance between us as much as possible.

"You're not my friend anymore!" she shouted, still shrouded by the trees. "You're dead! I'm coming after you! You're next!"

I picked up my pace and started running. Once I was out of the park, I continued running until I made my way to the subway station. I quickly showed my student pass as I ran to the platform. I knew that you weren't supposed to run on the platform because it was dangerous, but this was an emergency.

As soon as the train pulled into the station, I ran inside and sat down. My arms and legs were fidgeting; I couldn't keep still. I had to hurry and get home, so that I could warn Zoe.

Bathurst

"Hi, my name's John. Did you respond to the ad online too?" a burly man, wearing a t-shirt and ripped jeans, asked me.

Extending my hand towards him, I waited until he reciprocated the gesture. Shaking hands, I introduced myself. "Yes, I'm Casper. Nice to meet you."

"It's nice to meet you as well," John replied.

We were both standing inside the lobby of an apartment building. In the ad, we were instructed to wait here until someone came down to let us in. I was glad that I wasn't the only person who responded; I had been a little skeptical about interviewing for a prospective job at an apartment building.

I had noticed the ad a week ago, while mindlessly surfing online. There were very few details, but it had indicated that the pay rate was $15 an hour. Based on my recent bad luck with job hunting—I had been searching for a job for the past seven months—this seemed like an opportunity I couldn't refuse. Even if I had to scoop up cow dung with my bare hands, I would do it. I was desperate.

Looking around and taking in the building, I noticed that the lawn hadn't been mowed in a while. There were weeds growing, and unidentifiable items that had been long abandoned on the ground. The rest of the houses and buildings on the street were well maintained, so this building stood out. There were two cars parked across from the building. One of them looked like a normal car; the other looked like a total junker.

The door opened, and I quickly turned around to see who had entered. A nerdy and scrawny kid had come through the door, his gaze fixed on the ground. He quickly looked up a few times to see his surroundings, but his gaze quickly fell back to the ground.

"You're here for the job too?" I asked him.

He nodded his head, but didn't say anything. I couldn't be bothered to pry a verbal response from the kid, so I went back to letting my eyes wander around the building.

A few minutes later, a man came through the lobby's locked door. He had long black hair that hung just above his shoulders. He was wearing a green t-shirt and camouflage pants. His rundown combat boots were untied.

"You're here for the ad?" he asked, looking at each of us for a few seconds.

"Yes," John and I replied at the same time. I didn't hear the kid respond, but I assumed he just nodded.

"Follow me," the man said, leading us through the lobby door.

We followed him to a staircase, and climbed up three flights of stairs. Once we stepped foot into the hallway, there was a horrible stench. I couldn't identify it, and I didn't want to spend time trying to. Pinching my nose, I silently followed until we stopped in front of apartment number 3940.

Opening the door, he led us inside. I slowly let go of my nose, and was relieved that the smell didn't continue on into the apartment. We were ushered into the living room, and directed to take seats on the couch. John grabbed the only armchair, so I was stuck sitting on couch with the scrawny kid.

"To start things off, I would like to thank you for answering the ad I placed online. Allow me to introduce myself. I am Carl Webber-Bennett, and I have been tasked with recruiting individuals for our special operations division," Carl said.

"Wait a moment," I interjected. "I thought

this was a fifteen-bucks-an-hour job? Special operations division? That sounds like it should be taking in some hard cash."

Carl stared at me intently for a few seconds. I didn't know if his aim was to intimidate me. If it was, it wasn't working. No one could intimidate me.

"You must be Casper," he said, nodding his head. "In due time. As I was saying, you have been selected out of all applicants for this job. After conducting extensive background investigations on each of you, we have determined that you each possess qualities that will make you excel at this job."

Carl stopped talking, and looked to where the scrawny kid was sitting. Craning my neck to the side, I saw him with his hand up.

"You're not in school, nerd. Speak up if you need to talk," I said, shooting him a scatting look.

"I will have none of that," Carl said. "You are to respect everyone in this company, including the individuals in this room. At no point in time are you to use your bullying tactics on your colleagues. Save it for the job." He directed his attention back to the kid. "Brandon, go ahead."

"Sorry, sir. I just wanted to know what type of background check you performed. All I gave you was my name and email address. What exactly did you dig up on us?" Brandon asked.

"We have our ways," Carl replied. "In due time, you will learn our methods. You have nothing to fear, unless of course you choose to not accept the job you have been offered."

"So, you're threatening us?" I interjected again. "You really think the way to recruit people is to threaten them to take the job, otherwise you'll do something to them? You're full of yourself. What's your company's name anyways? Jerkwads?"

"Each of you possess skills that are needed to succeed in what we do," he continued, ignoring my question. Before I can divulge any information about our company or your roles, I need you to accept the job that was offered to you. I know that you may be a bit skeptical of signing your name to a contract, without knowing what it is you are agreeing to. We urge you to put faith in the matter at hand, and believe that it will be worth it."

I looked around the room. Brandon was squirming on the couch, while John remained silent and stoic. I couldn't tell what he was thinking, and he hadn't opened his mouth once to say anything.

"You know, what the hell. I'm in. Where do I

sign up to this crap?" I said. I might as well go for it. Fifteen dollars was fifteen dollars, after all.

"I'll sign the contract as well, sir," Brandon said.

Carl silently handed us a piece of paper. I didn't bother reading it, and signed my name to the bottom of the page. The contract wouldn't be telling me anything more than he already had.

"John, have you decided? Will you sign the contract?" Carl asked him. I was pissed off that he was nice and gentle with him. Where was the attitude he had given me?

Extending his hand out, John grabbed the contract Carl had extended towards him. He looked over it for a second, signed his name, and handed it back over to him. "There you go, boss."

We all watched as Carl carefully checked the contracts, and then placed them in a folder. He disappeared for a few minutes into another room. When he came back, he was carrying a crate that appeared to weight a ton, based on how he was struggling with it.

The crate made a thud as he dropped it on the ground. Stepping onto it with his right leg, he rested his elbow on his knee.

"It looks like we're just about ready to start, recruits. First things first: we need to clarify a few things. You will not be getting paid $15 an hour. If we had placed any other amount, we would have received applicants that most likely would not have been suitable for the job. Your rate of pay will be $25 an hour during training, and then it will increase to $40 an hour once you start engaging in active missions.

"You are now working for the Nation Recovery Company. NRC, for short. On paper your cheques will be made out from Albasco-Yuts Data Processing Inc., but make no mistake about it: you are working for NRC now. You are not to disclose our name or our mission to anyone, including your close friends and family. As far as they know, you're paper pushers at a data-processing company. Keep it simple.

"We will begin training tomorrow. We will meet back here bright and early at six in the morning. You will be issued a basic training pack. Open it, familiarize yourself with it, and practice putting it on. When you come in tomorrow, show up in your civilian clothing. Got it?"

I nodded, taking everything in. I didn't hear

anyone else talking, so I assumed they had nodded like I had. I was curious to know what was in that crate. It looked like my curiosity would soon be answered, as Carl removed his leg from the crate and bent down to open it.

Without saying a word, he took out a black duffel bag from the crate. As he handed it over to Brandon, I could see his name stitched on it. The second one he retrieved was given to me, and the last one was given to John. I ran my hand over my stitched name, before turning my attention back to Carl.

"That's it for today. You'll find a signing bonus in your bags. Don't worry, it won't be reported on your taxes. You'll be getting paid in cash until your training is done. Once you become active, we'll add you to the payroll. Any question?" Carl asked.

No one said anything. I remained quiet, mostly because I had nothing to say. Carl walked over to the front door of the apartment, and opened it up. Taking the hint, we all got up and walked out the door. I followed the other two down the staircase, and ditched them once we left the building. I wasn't in the mood for any small talk.

I walked as fast as I could, eager to get home.

I couldn't wait to see what was in the bag. That Carl guy was talking some crazy stuff, but I could deal with crazy. I still didn't understand why they picked Brandon to join, but who the hell cares?

As soon as I saw the sign for the subway station, I jogged until I reached the entrance. Paying my fare, I pushed through the turnstile and made my way to the platform. Letting my eagerness get the best of me, I dropped my bag to the floor and crouched down to open it.

As I opened my bag, I quickly closed it and made sure that no one was near me. Opening up the flap partially—I didn't want to get caught on the cameras—I admired the assault rifle that was prominently displayed on top of what appeared to be a military uniform. Beside it, there was a manila envelope. I opened the envelope, and let out a sigh of excitement: there was at least a thousand dollars in there. The envelope was full of $100 bills.

The train entered the station, making a lot of noise. I closed my bag, and double checked that the zipper was sealed all the way to the end. Getting onto the train, I sat down and propped my feet on the opposing seat. As the train departed the station, a smile crept onto my face. I couldn't wait to see what tomorrow had in store.

Spadina

I was running late for my appointment. I had initially arrived early, but I lost track of time. I had walked over to the nearby coffee shop, and settled myself into a chair with today's paper and a steaming cup of delicious caffeinated goodness. Afraid of being late, I quickly gulped down the remainder of my coffee and dropped my empty cup into the garbage, as I flew out the door.

Luckily for me, the doctor's office wasn't too far away. I was fairly confident I would still make my appointment, even though I was technically already ten minutes late. They made me wait all the time; now it was their turn.

As I arrived at the office, I swung the door open and made my way to the receptionist. It took her a few minutes before she even acknowledged my existence.

"Can I help you?" she asked, in a nasally voice.

"Yes, I have an appointment with Dr. Carlin," I replied.

She extended her hand out, but didn't say

anything. It took me a few seconds to realize she must be asking for my health card. Fishing it out of my wallet, I handed it to her.

"You're late," she said.

"Indeed, I am. Sorry about that," I replied.

She confirmed my name, date of birth, and address, and told me to go sit in the waiting area. I turned around and made my way towards the waiting area. There was an old man and two young women already seated. I took a seat away from them, preferring to wait in solitary peace.

In my rush getting here, I had forgotten to bring my paper with me. It was probably being enjoyed by some lucky soul at the coffee shop. Oh, what I would give to be inhaling the sweet smell of freshly ground coffee beans.

I looked around the room, and noticed a pile of magazines on a small table. Getting up from my seat, I perused the pile until I landed on one that looked mildly interesting. As I headed back to my seat, I noticed the old man repeatedly glancing in my direction.

Sitting down, I opened the magazine and flipped over to the first page that had more than a paragraph worth of words on it. Halfway through the article, I could feel eyes burning into me. Glancing up from the magazine and focusing my attention on him, I looked him directly in the eyes. I propped the corners of my mouth into a smile, and waved at him.

"Why in the hell are you waving to me, boy?" the old man asked.

Taken aback, I quickly lowered my hand and brought it to my side. "I was just trying to be friendly, sir. I noticed you looking my way, so..." I allowed my words to trail off, not knowing what else to say.

"I don't need no fairy boy like you waving at me. Are you a fairy? You sure look like one," he retorted. There was so much anger drawn on his face.

At this point, I didn't know whether I should laugh or be offended. Frankly, I was taken aback by what was coming out of this old man's mouth. And to think he looked so innocent and frail when I walked in. Deciding to ignore him, I returned my attention to my magazine.

"Hey, boy! Don't you hear me talking to you!" he shouted across the room. At this point, the two women were covertly catching glances of us, while pretending to be engrossed in their phones.

I looked up from the magazine once more, and shot him a forced smile. "I sure do!" I exclaimed.

"What can I do for you?"

"You can start by telling me how two upstanding Canadians made such a sissy boy. You're probably one of them Europeans. That explains it," he said.

There was no stopping the confrontation with him now. "Why yes, born and bred. I'll be sure to let my parents know of your constructive criticism. If we're lucky, maybe we'll catch them just in time so that my brother doesn't end up like that either."

I stared at the man, looking him straight in the eyes. He wasn't going to bully me.

"Oh, so now you're joking around. Do you think I'm playing with you, boy?" he asked.

I chuckled. "It sounds like you're stuck back in the olden days, and you've somehow mistaken my identity with that of one of your old bullying victims. Was there something in particular I could help you with?"

The old man kissed his teeth, which echoed loudly in the waiting room. I watched as he grabbed his cane and made his way towards me. He hovered above me for a few seconds, before taking a seat across from me.

"Do you go to church?" he asked me.

"I think we've previously established that I was a heathen, no? I'm guessing the answer would be pretty self-explanatory then," I replied. A part of me wanted to escape this abuse, but another part wanted to see just how far this man would go.

"This is what you need to do, unless you want your soul to burn in hell for eternity. You need to go to church, go to confession, and ask God for forgiveness," he replied.

"What do I need forgiveness for? I guess I could ask him to forgive me for lying to my friend. You see, she had asked if her haircut was nice. It wasn't; it looked like she had a mullet. Tempted by sin, I lied and told her I liked it. Damn it, I'm going to hell," I said, throwing him a sneer.

"Boy, you think this is funny, uh? You really think this is funny? You need to ask God to forgive you for all that fairy behaviour you engage in. Fornicating with other men! Atrocious!" he exclaimed.

I tried to keep my cool. It took everything within me to not lunge across and hit him in the face. I couldn't believe the two women and the receptionist were acting like nothing was happening. You'd think at the very least the receptionist would do something.

"Why aren't you answering me, boy? I'm talking to you. Didn't your mama ever teach you to respect your elders?" he said, his eyes filled with rage. His face was shaking from the intensity of his anger.

I let out a sigh. "I was under the impression that respect was for everyone, not just the elderly. And what was that other bit she told me? I think it was something along the lines of respect being earned. Does that sound right to you?" I said to him.

I watched as he continued shaking in his chair, engulfed by rage. Watching him was funny and sad at the same time. I was conflicted between showing this man sympathy for his clearly backwards and rage-filled thinking, or showing him anger for the way he had been treating me from the moment I had sat down in the waiting area.

"Sir, did I do something to offend you?" I asked him, trying to deescalate the situation.

"You know what will do you some good? What will turn you back onto the path of God? You should go out with my granddaughter, Blanche. Her no-good boyfriend left her because of supposed attitude problems. I can assure you she has no attitude problems. She takes after her granddaddy. That should put you back on the path to God. You can have a wife, kids, and give up that man on man fornication," he said.

I have had just about enough. "You know what? I've been as patient and as courteous as possible towards you. I wouldn't touch your granddaughter if she was the last woman on earth, especially if she takes after you. You are a bigoted vile old man. I hope karma treats you kindly," I said to him.

Getting up from my seat, I went to the receptionist. She ignored me for a few minutes before finally looking away from her computer. I asked her if she could do something about the way the old man was acting, but she merely shrugged and told me that he had an appointment.

Instead of going back into the waiting room, I remained standing near the receptionist's desk. I didn't want to be here any longer, but I wasn't going to let a vile old man make me miss my appointment. After another five minutes of waiting, I was called into the doctor's office.

The doctor rushed through my appointment, but I didn't even care. As soon as I was done, I immediately left the building. I didn't bother glancing into the waiting room. If I caught sight of him again, I would most likely do something that would end up with me sitting in jail. That piece of crap wasn't worth it.

As I walked towards the subway station, I took out my phone and tried calling my girlfriend. She didn't pick up, and it went straight to voicemail. I tried calling again, but it still didn't go through. As I entered the subway station, I tried once more to no avail.

Waiting on the platform, I leaned against the wall and closed my eyes. Today was such a good day, and that man had perverted it. I felt like punching something, letting all of my rage out. As the train pulled into the station, I opened my eyes.

Getting onto the train, I sat down and contemplated my day. I was originally going to head over to the mall, but now I just wanted to go home. As the train pulled away from the station, I closed my eyes and imagined him burning in the pits of hell, along with his granddaughter, Blanche.